The Secret of the Space Scrolls

and

Cholent

St. Helier, Jersey

The Secret of the Space Scrolls

by Gideon Marc

Contents

Chapter 1

Follow Those Aliens!

The servo-sign in front of Benji suddenly turned bright green. Startled, he dropped the small bag he had been clutching. It fell onto the carpet, hitting Esti's foot.

"It's only an announcement," his sister told him, laughing, as the spaceport lounge emptied of humans, off-worlders, and androids hurriedly boarding a Venusian shuttle.

Esti picked up the blue bag with gold embroidery and put it on the table. "What kind of off-world writing is this?" she asked looking at the strange markings on the bag.

"Hey! Let go!" Benji commanded, grabbing the bag from his sister. "This isn't off-world writing. This is Hebrew, dummy."

"So it's Hebrew. Who cares?" she answered, aware that she should have known what the letters were. After all, she had had 7 years of Hebrew School study, right up to her 12th birthday. "And anyway," she continued, trying to excuse her ignorance, "it's script Hebrew not print."

"Forget it!" Benji mumbled, wanting to change the subject.

Esti didn't. "Why didn't you send it with the rest of the luggage?" she asked.

"Because," retorted Benji.

"Because why?"

"Because I didn't."

"The way you hold onto that bag anyone would think you found the secret of the universe."

"Maybe it is the secret of the universe," he said defiantly.

His sister gave him a withering look. "Saturn's rings! What are you talking about?"

"Have you seen what's inside?"

"I don't have to."

"They are very, very old."

"Benji, our zeydeh is very, very old. That's another secret of the universe, I suppose."

"You're only jealous because he trusted *me* to bring them."

"Do you know what you are, Benji? In Grampsspeak, meshuggah!"

Before Benji could reply there was a commotion

in the lounge. A couple of robo-tendees seemed to have gone out of control. They were whirling around, throwing cakes and cookies in all directions. People began shouting as the missiles hit with robot-like precision.

Benji and Esti couldn't help laughing.

"This is fun," said Benji, ducking as a cherry pie landed in his sister's face. Carefully placing the bag on his seat, Benji picked up a hard roll and threw it at one of the robots. To his surprise, the robot whizzed it back. Benji caught the roll and pitched it back. The robo-tendee copied his exact motions. Soon they were pitching to each other as food swirled around them.

Benji was so engrossed in his game he didn't notice when all the robo-tendees suddenly went limp; all, that is, except for the one he was pitching to and another robot who had quietly taken the blue bag off his chair.

Esti was still wiping her face when she caught a glimpse of the robot speeding past, clutching the bag. "Benji, the bag!" she yelled out.

Benji gave chase but the robo-tendee was well past him. Taking aim, Benji pitched the hard roll he had been playing with directly at the runaway robot. It landed low, between the robot's legs. Slightly off balance, the robot careened down the main hallway smashing into everything in its path. Robo-cleaners were knocked over, hovercarts were sent spinning like 20th-century bumper-cars, and droid-pets ran howling as their owners tried to turn them off.

Through the din Benji kept shouting, "Stop! Stop thief!" But no one could hear him.

The robot reached the end of the hallway and scurried through the exit. As Benji followed he looked out of the giant plasty windows, hoping to see where the robot was headed. When he saw its destination, his heart sank. The robot was travelling toward an alien spacecraft.

Wait a minute, Benji told himself. That's not possible. Robots can't leave their place of work. Everyone knows that. Droids! I've got him now, Benji smiled as he closed the gap between them.

Just as Benji had suspected, the robot was standing at the edge of the spaceport perimeter, careful not to step over the laser lights that marked its outer boundary.

But the bag! Where was the bag? The robot was emptyhanded! And the spaceship was jetting! Benji rushed towards the craft but was stopped by an explosive flash. "Droids!" he exclaimed, his mouth opening wide. The robot's head had liquidized. A heat ray was systematically melting what was left of the robot. Molten metal oozed from its open neck. It was visibly shrinking as the sizzling drops streamed down its body.

Just above his head, Benji spotted the yellow

Benji kept shouting, "Stop! Stop thief!"

hue of a tractor beam sending his grandfather's bag toward the open portal of the alien craft. A scaly hand suddenly appeared and snatched the bag as the craft sped away.

Benji's speaksee was beeping. Esti's face filled the screen. He pressed the R-button. "Benji, what's happening?" she asked, frantically.

A crowd was gathering, uniformed men approaching, and his big sister was calling. Benji realized that he had to follow the spaceship. His folks would be mad. But he had promised Zeydeh.

He pushed through the crowd and jumped into a cab which, strangely, seemed to have been waiting for him. He pointed at the rising dust trail ahead and said, "Follow that alien...I mean that ship."

"What ship?" asked the cabby, glancing at the dozens of spacecraft zooming overhead.

Benji pointed again, only this time at the control panel. "There, that one!" he shouted, hoping the spacefinder on this old cab was as accurate as it should be. The alien craft had zoomed up to the stratosphere and was hovering. That made it easy to spot.

"Okay, kid," said the cabby, as he sped off. "Let's have your John Hancock."

"What?" replied Benji, puzzled, seeing part of the panel light up.

"Authorization input, kid. Which finger did

they byte?"

"Oh, the little finger on the right," said Benji, passing a ring over the area flashing blue.

"Benji!"

In the rush and excitement he had forgotten his sister. Her voice and face screamed at him from the speaksee. "Don't you dare leave the spaceport! Forget Gramps' silly old bag! Get out of that cab and come back now! This is no time for games, understand?"

"Sis, some mutant took the bag and turned the robot into cholent mush. I'm hot on its trail, and I'm going to get Gramps' bag back."

Benji saw his sister's face contorting in rage but before she could say another word he pressed the mute button. "Sorry, Sis," he said with a sly grin.

Chapter 2
Ne Peppered!

They were slowly inching their way toward the alien craft, the cabby totally indifferent to Benji's constant prodding.

"Faster, faster!" Benji shouted, bouncing in his seat and pounding on the armrests.

"Don't worry, kid, we'll catch her. You just relax and enjoy the ride. Talmon's my name. Want a cigar?"

"Are you nuts? I'm ten years old."

"How about a whiskey?"

"No."

"Juice?"

"Not now."

"Lollipop?"

"Look, can't we go any faster?" Benji asked,

frustrated.

"So what's your problem?" the cabby wondered, switching to auto-pilot and reaching under his seat for a bottle marked "Old Screech Rum". He took a swig and leaned back.

"Where are you from?" he called, looking half-asleep.

"New Earth," Benji answered, beginning to worry about this slightly drunk cabby.

"And where you going?"

"Well, if you ever catch up to those robbers, I hope to get back my zeydeh's tefillin in time to give it to him on Pesach."

"Whoa there. Your what's what? In time for what?"

Benji slowly explained. "They've got my grandfather's prayers...uh...boxes...symbols and I have to get them back by the Jewish holiday called Passover. Is that clear?" He was getting more and more annoyed.

"Almost," grinned the cabby.

"Will you go faster, please?" begged Benji.

"Cab rules. No speeding in town. Sci-fi mags are under the seat."

"Droids!" muttered Benji to himself. "I've got a madman for a cabby."

"Hey, I heard that, kid," responded Talmon smartly. "I'll have you know that I am one of only 14,000 cabbies on this planet allowed to ferry interstellar passengers. What do you think of that?"

Benji couldn't resist. "14,000 you say. Well, how many cabbies are there on this planet?" he asked, repressing a smile.

"Don't be a wise groid," the cabby smirked, taking another swig from his bottle. "And, I'll have you know that this here cab is the latest antediluvian model. She's got bust thrust, alert skirts, fleet feet, wise eyes, dream beams, mean screens, bright bytes, code modes, and lots more."

For the first time Benji saw Talmon become animated.

"Best of all are the weapons on this baby," the cabby bragged.

"Weapons?" As far as Benji knew only short-fire lasers were allowed on cabs, the kind that could squeech a rogue drapper or a flying gratlik. He never heard of a fully armed cab.

"Why, I can do things that would make your hair stand on end."

"I think I've had enough hair standing on end for one day," Benji confided. "Let's just keep moving."

Talmon became more talkative as he drank. The cab was doing over 500 mph, but the alien spaceship had begun to leave the pull of the planet and was heading out into open space. Benji was sure that once the aliens left their New Earth orbit he would never see his zeydeh's bag again.

"Well, Mr. Talmon, I ..."

"Talmon, kid, just Talmon," the cabby said. Then as though reading Benji's mind, "And don't worry, I never lose a ship, or a fare. Where they go, I go. This baby can do 2,000 klicks in open space. I even had a warp wand put in her just in case I ever need to leave town in a hurry, if you get my klitsch. By the way kid, what's your name?"

"Benji, Benji Kohen," Benji told him, wondering who this Talmon really was. "How did you get a warp wand? I thought only the galacties and priority spaceships were allowed wands."

"Hey, Benji, stop worrying so much. My motto is ne peppered!" Talmon said, slurring his words.

"Be prepared, you mean. The old Boy Scout motto," Benji corrected.

"I said what I mean. Ne peppered! That's the motto of the Saurian Slave Runners on Gamma 5. It means something like those Boy Scout words only... only... more prepared. How old is your zaid, anyway?" asked Talmon, a little confused himself.

"Zeydeh," Benji corrected. "He's 115 years old. He asked me to keep this special bag for him. It's the only thing he ever asked of me, and now I zoffed it.

"Maybe my sister is right. Maybe we should head back home and let the police take care of it. I probably wouldn't be able to get the bag back even if we catch the crooks."

"Police! COPS! Why they can't catch anything,

not even a cold. Half of them are droids and the other half ought to be. Me, I believe if you want to get something done, do it yourself. Of course, having enough fire power helps, if you get my klitsch. Now, why don't you just relax," Talmon advised his passenger, pressing the recline button on Benji's seat. "At this rate we won't catch up to them for about six hours. Grab some sleep. We'll get those weirdos, trust me, we'll get them." Talmon leaned over the control panel and pressed a button.

Something strange happened, because before Benji knew it, he was fast asleep.

Chapter 3
What's A Mayven?

When Benji awoke it was to find himself face to face with a pair of blood red cat's eyes. The rest of the jet black cat was perched comfortably on his lap.

"Hey, Talmon," Benji said, shaking the cabby, who was blissfully snoring. "How did this black thing get in here?" he asked.

"I am not a thing," said the creature, with mild reproach. "I am a cat, and I have been here all the time."

"I didn't see you."

"That is because I am a cautious cat."

"Anyway, you're illegal," said Benji, unsure as to whether or not he should stroke the cat. "Pet-droids aren't supposed to talk."

"Hey Talmon, how did this black thing get in here?"

"Wro-ong, kid," said Talmon, yawning. "Seya is not a pet or a droid. She is from the cat planet, Fellini."

"Never heard of it," said Benji.

"Oh, it's light years away," said Seya, licking herself.

"Her wicked uncle cast her off in a sleep pod," explained Talmon. "By pure luck I happened to be passing and now we're a team. I can tell you kid, she's a very handy cat to have around, especially when you're facing trouble."

Benji didn't know if he believed Talmon. Who could tell with this strange character and his wild stories?

"Okay," said Benji, "so what great wonders can she do?"

"Well, one thing I can do," said the cat, leaping from Benji's lap onto Talmon's shoulder, "is to warn you that in 10 seconds we are going to be attacked."

"Action stations. Fasten up, kid," said Talmon, activating his shields. "Now you know what I mean by ne peppered."

From out of nowhere tracer balls of fire came streaking across the sky straight at them. Benji was sure they would be a hit. But, miraculously, the balls just bounced away.

"Now it's my turn," said Talmon, with a grim smile.

But Benji didn't hear any return fire. Talmon

was scanning, but he had not yet locked onto a target. Where had the attack come from, Benji wondered.

"What the ..." began Talmon, but before he could say more a tremendous explosion rocked the cab, sending it into a spin. Benji was feeling sick. The cab straightened for a second, long enough for Benji to see they had broken through clouds and were hurtling down towards the ground of a strange alien planet. If Talmon didn't do something quickly they would crash into the mountain below.

In a rasping voice Talmon was saying, "Come on baby, come on baby," over and over, willing the cab to pull out of the dive.

Suddenly there was a jolt. Benji felt as though he would be catapulted out of his seat, but his straps held. The cab had straightened.

"Attack from behind," warned the cat.

With a roar, the cab somersaulted behind the attackers.

"Now I've got you," Talmon sneered, and fired. Three blaster beams converged on the tail of the enemy ship. Smoke poured out and it dropped like a stone. Two figures ejected just before the ship hit the ground.

Benji couldn't contain his excitement. "Look, Talmon," he said straining in his seat. "One of them just dropped something."

Talmon brought the cab down near where the

bandits had landed.

Benji rushed out first with Seya following. Just ahead a familiar object was lying near the mouth of a cave.

Benji ran forward ignoring the cat's warning to stop. A stun ray cut across his path.

"Bring the kid back," Talmon called to Seya from the cab. "It's too dangerous."

"Go back," hissed Seya when she caught up with Benji. "I'll try and grab the bag. They may not see me."

Benji rejoined Talmon. Together they watched the cat circle slowly to get within striking distance.

Talmon brought out his laz-gun.

"Are they aliens or droids?" whispered Benji.

"Don't know yet," Talmon admitted.

The cat was only jumping distance from her prey. They saw her hunch then spring. As she was halfway into the air a scaly hand appeared from nowhere whipping Seya aside. The gnarled green hand grabbed the blue bag and suddenly disappeared from view. Before anyone had a chance to do anything a space bike burst out of the cave. Its prehistoric looking rider held Benji's bag firmly in its alien grip. Just as it was almost out of sight Talmon opened fire. Much too late.

Then Benji saw Talmon talking earnestly into the cab's speaker-mike for a couple of minutes.

"Okay, kid," he said to Benji. "This is the situation. The cab is not battle fit and our scaly friend may return, so it's not safe for you here. We are on Ichsa Planet, and down the mountain is Junka City. I have a good friend there. He is an outcast but he will look after you. His name is Vitch – an inventive whiz and a little mad. I just spoke to him and he knows all about your zeydeh's bag."

"What do you mean he knows all about the bag?"

"You'll see when you meet him."

"But how will I find him?"

"Seya will take you."

"And what about you?"

"I'll catch up with you later, kid. That's a promise, okay?"

"Come on Benji," said the cat.

The path down the mountain was wide enough for cats, but not humans. Benji felt like a tightrope walker as he carefully balanced himself with his hands outstretched. Step by slow step he followed Seya down the winding path.

"How much further? he asked her, panting.

"About 10 minutes."

They came to a bend and then the path widened. As though to make up for the ease with which Benji could now walk, a bumper crop of garbage served as an obstacle course for both Benji and the cat. Muck and rubbish were everywhere piled high, as if a dozen dumpsters had unloaded their putrid contents along the trail.

Further ahead Benji could see abandoned pods, cabs, shuttles, trackers, cruisers, and platform stations. All types of machinery of every shape and color were strewn about in heaps over a vast area as far as the eye could see.

"No wonder they call it Junka City," said Benji.

"I call it Junka City Jungle."

"Jungle? Are there animals here?"

Seya laughed. "Oh yes, there are animals. Just watch."

"I don't understand," Benji said nervously, straining to spot a wild animal, and at the same time, hoping he didn't see one. "I don't see anything moving."

"You will," said the cat.

As they got closer to the valley floor Benji saw that the city was indeed alive, with noisy activity. Pet-droids of unimaginable variety were either running or fighting. The grunting, growling, barking, snarling, squawking, squealing and screaming were ear-splitting.

Seya sprang onto Benji's shoulder. "Hide," she hissed into his ear.

The closest shelter was an old jetpod hanging precariously on a sloping heap of crushed shuttles. As Benji climbed in through the window, the wreck began to teeter.

"Quick," the cat whispered frantically. "Whatever you do don't let them see us."

"Huh?" Benji asked, but the cat was already curled at the bottom of the pod. Following her lead, he huddled near her.

After a few moments of nothing more exciting than the sounds of rats scuttling through the wrecks Benji decided to look out the pod's smashed window. What he saw made him freeze. Screeters! Two of them. Their leathery bodies glistened green as they kept their long, pointed snouts sniffing into the wind. They had three rows of sharp, pointed teeth, with an extra row designed just for ripping. They were dedicated hunters, never giving up on a prey until it was killed. Officially, anyone who saw a screeter was legally-bound to shoot it. Unofficially, anyone who saw a screeter made sure it did not see him. Fortunately, for Benji, the screeters were chasing a Jovian grafaleg.

In open terrain the grafaleg might have stood a chance. Grafalegs resembled giant tigers, except that they had a long row of feathery horns along their backs. The horns were nature's way of assuring their survival. When the grafaleg ran, its horns flattened into hundreds of short feathers that caught the air and gave the creature lift. Were it not so heavy, the grafaleg would have been able to fly. As it was it could run faster than any known animal in the universe. Flat out, grafalegs could do 140 mph for up to 22 minutes!

But here, zigzagging and jumping over all the litter, the grafaleg was doomed.

One screeter disappeared from view as the grafaleg galloped blindly towards their pod. Suddenly, there was a thump on top of the cabin. The screeter! The pod tilted as the creature settled in. Benji almost stopped breathing. Sweat poured down his back. His heart was pumping away. Then he heard tiny scraping sounds. He forced himself to look up and saw the screeter's monstrous black claws curling over the edge of the window. The cabin groaned and lurched some more. Then the screeter leaped.

The grafaleg saw the screeter ahead of it but there was little it could do. Its snarl seemed wasted as the screeter opened its enormous mouth. Then it emitted a high-pitched scream which seemed to stun the grafaleg. By the time it recovered the screeter was on it, ripping and tearing at the hapless animal. The second screeter came onto the scene and immediately both creatures began to fight. Benji didn't want to wait around to be dessert for the winner.

He and Seya jumped out of the pod and ran for what seemed like hours. Exhausted, Benji lay down near a strange looking spacecraft with the word "Hashem" written on nearly every inch of its surface.

"Get ready," Seya told him.

"Get ready for what?" Benji asked, out of breath. "Give me a chance to rest and then I'll be ready for anything this crazy planet can throw at us. But my feet are killing me. I've just got to –"

Suddenly, a circle of light engulfed him and the next thing Benji saw was a tall man with white hair flowing from underneath a wide-brimmed black hat. He wore a long beard and an old-fashioned black suit. "Welcome aboard," he greeted them from the ship's doorway. "I'm Vitch," he smiled.

Benji picked himself up and walked over to Vitch. The old man put out his hand and Benji took it, more to get a lift into the ship than to shake hands. Pushing aside some containers, Vitch led his guests to the rear of the ship.

"Is this the fellow Talmon told us to look for?" Benji whispered to Seya.

"It is," Seya replied.

"Talmon said you could help us," Benji said out loud, not feeling too comfortable amid the clutter and disarray.

Bending down, Vitch placed his hands on Benji's shoulders and faced him squarely. "Boychick," he said kindly, "I know all about your problems and I think I can help. But first let's ask Mayven what he thinks."

"Mayven?" Benji echoed looking around. There was no one else in the room but the two of them and

Suddenly, a circle of light engulfed him...

the cat.

"Mayven!" Vitch called out to no one in particular, "are you awake?"

"Awake," said a grainy voice which Benji now understood must be Vitch's computer. "Mincha in twenty minutes," the computer announced.

"Thanks Mayven," Vitch said. Then, turning to Benji he asked, "Do you know what mincha is, Benji?"

"Mincha?" Benji repeated, startled by the question. He took a moment to think and then said, "Mincha is afternoon prayers, isn't it?"

"Did you hear that, Mayven?" Vitch yelled at his computer, "There's hope for the future yet. A talmid chochom, a scholar in residence!" He was absolutely beaming. Then, lowering his voice he said to the computer, "Now, let's get it right the first time. Prepare to take off for Rattatat 5."

"Preparing for lift off," the computer replied as the ship's jets began to glow.

"What's Rattatty 5?" Benji asked, wondering if it was such a good idea to travel in this Junka City spaceship.

"Rattatat 5," Vitch corrected. "Arry Abadan's there," he said, taking his seat at the helm. "He's a crooked art dealer. Steals ancient treasures, artifacts, anything to turn a profit."

"Is Rattawhateveryoucallit far?"

"Mayven, tell Benji how far it is to Rattatat 5

from Junka City."

"About 17 minutes," replied the computer, "plus another 7 for mincha."

Vitch swung round in his chair. "Well, boychick, are you ready?"

"Ready," Benji answered, trying to smile, "but after mincha no stopping for maariv."

He saw Seya's puzzled look. "That's evening prayers, Seya," he told her, winking at Vitch.

Vitch laughed. "Benji, my boy," he said, reaching over and patting his head, "you've got a sense of humor. I like that, as long as you watch the chutzpah. We may make a mensch out of you yet, right Mayven?"

"Right as raygin", said Mayven. "Now, where was it we were going again, Rattatat Hive?"

"Not you too," Vitch shouted. "Rattatat 5!" both he and Benji called out in unison.

"Senile silicon," muttered Seya.

Twenty-five minutes later Mayven announced that they were in orbit around Rattatat 5.

Vitch gave Benji a piece of glistening tape.

"It's a message-strip," he told him. "Twist it around your finger. When you want to communicate with me, Seya or Mayven, just snap your fingers. It's tuned to our message-strips and Mayven's special frequency."

"In case we get separated," Seya told him as they prepared to land.

Chapter 4
Eggscuse! Eggscuse!

They landed in a huge, dirty, silver-domed com-
plex. Hundreds of spacecraft filled the bays,
mostly pods, space-cars, cabs and hoppers.

They took a cab to the center of the city. The
streets were smelly, filthy and noisy. Alien urchins
darted in and out from murky holes like moles.

As they got out of the cab Vitch warned Benji,
"Watch your pockets. The Rattatat street kids can
steal the schmaltz from between two slices of bread
without ever opening the sandwich."

"Huh?" Benji asked, wondering what Vitch was
talking about.

"Just be careful," hissed Seya.

In the market area shops and stalls were ablaze
with color. Toys and games sprang to life as Benji

approached. "Hold me, love me, I'm your friend," said an array of dolls. "Kill! Kill!" blared clawed mechanical monsters that showed their teeth.

Suddenly, a real clawed hand grabbed Vitch by the ear, pulling him into a stall. Benji was rooted to the spot.

"Hallo Vitch," said a scraggly-haired old woman with black saucer eyes on both sides of her head. Did you think I wouldn't see you, dearie?" she cackled, releasing her grip and licking her talons.

"No, no," said Vitch, a little shaken. "Nothing passes your pretty faces."

"Do I please *Him*?" she asked.

"Very much," Vitch answered. "I was going to pay you a visit later. I have to escort my young friend here on a mission."

"One of *His* missions?" the old lady inquired. "Can I help?"

"No. I mean yes, one of His missions but no you can't help."

Seeing her dejected look, Vitch added, "But I hear that among your clan you have brought peace between those who would quarrel, and truth where only darkness ruled. Is that true?"

"Yes," said the hag, pulling open a small drawer. "Here is the secret you have shared with me. I keep it close."

Benji couldn't believe his ears. Secret? Zeydeh's bag! He moved closer to Vitch.

The old woman held up a holobook that looked surprisingly like the Bible Benji had studied in Hebrew School. Was she Jewish? he wondered.

"That's wonderful," said Vitch, shaking his head and smiling, "but now we must go." Taking Benji's hand he rushed outside.

"Who was she?" asked Benji as they hurried away.

"A witch," said Vitch.

"A witch?" Benji echoed.

"Her kind are called witches because that's how they look. Of course, they're not really witches, and among her clan she's considered quite beautiful. Some time ago she expressed a curiosity about Judaism and before I knew it she'd decided to join our people. After two years of study, she is almost ready to become a full-fledged Jewess. Needless to say, she's quite enthusiastic and sincere."

"She sure is," Benji mumbled to himself. There was more to this Vitch than met the eye, Benji thought.

As they walked further they came to a mall. Entering the dome-like structure, Benji couldn't help but feel that they were being watched, maybe even followed. When he told Vitch, the old man just shrugged and said, "Here everyone follows everyone else. It's the way things are. Everyone expects it. But don't worry, Seya will give us plenty of warning if someone gets too close. Right, my feline friend?"

In answer, Seya climbed onto Vitch's shoulder and gave his beard a lick. Then she jumped down and continued to lead the way.

Vitch paused by a holosign which showed a man with six mouths drinking some liquid. The sign said:

YOUR FIRST DRINKS FREE!
MULTI-MOUTHS WELCOME!

"I'm going inside to ask around," Vitch told them. "You and Seya wait for me here."

Benji looked at the assortment of weird humanoids just hanging around outside. Some had animal heads and human bodies, and some had human heads with animal-like bodies. All were part of the sinister underworld that made its home on Rattatat 5. It gave him the creeps.

Seya pushed her face into Benji's ear and said gently, "Don't show any fear. Vitch is already on his way back."

Vitch came out at that very moment. "Okay," he told them. "Arry Abadan was here about three hours ago and then left to meet his cronies in the Crybian corner. That's where he makes his deals. Follow me. Stay close," he advised.

The three of them reached an exotic little garden in the middle of the mall. More unsavory aliens were sitting, huddled around small glowing picnic tables.

"This is the place," said Vitch.

Benji looked at the strange faces. "What does Arry look like?" he asked.

"He's a Mishmashan," said Vitch. "They are from a planet of mutants with human bodies and animal heads, like those three in the corner."

Benji could see what looked like a bearhead, a lionhead and a foxhead.

"Arry has the head of a donkey," Vitch told him. "He's hard to miss."

"We must hurry," Seya suddenly warned. "I intuit that a number of extremely bad things are going to happen here very soon."

Vitch did not take Seya's warning lightly. "From what I understand your hunches have saved more lives than my grandmother's chicken soup," he complimented her. "Okay, let's find out who's been in contact with Arry. Benji, see those egg-shaped beings over there?" Vitch pointed to a group of Humpty-Dumpty like creatures. "You take Seya and see if you can find out anything. I'll deal with the Mishmashans."

Seya led the way to the first of the Eggis.

"Excuse me, sir," said Benji. The Eggi ignored Benji completely.

"Excuse me," Benji said more forcefully. The Eggi continued to ignore him.

Very gently, Benji leaned over and tapped the Eggi near the top of his head. He heard a hollow sound. "Excuse me, sir!" he almost shouted.

The Eggi swivelled totally around. "Eggscuse! Eggscuse!" he squeaked. "Can't you see we're eggstremely busy. Speak up! Be eggsplicit and eggsplain what you want."

"Sorry, sir," said Benji, slightly overwhelmed. "Uh, I'm looking for Arry Abadan, I ..."

"Say no more, boy," the Eggi told him. "Arry eggsited twenty minutes eggo. But judging by his eggcited eggspression, he wasn't egging to go."

"Thanks," Benji cried out, as he rushed to find Vitch. Seya trailed close behind. She didn't have time to tell Benji about the anthropoid leg that jutted out, deliberately tripping the boy. Benji fell forward, landing on the brick floor, hard.

By the time Seya caught up to him a strong hairy hand had picked up Benji and was shaking him in the air. Benji opened his eyes and saw a giant rat staring at him. It was a Mishmashan.

"What's your hurry, little earthling?" asked rathead, examining the boy closely. Everyone nearby was laughing.

"Let me go, let me go," shouted Benji, struggling to free himself. "Let me go now!" he yelled at the top of his voice.

"Good lungs, wouldn't you say?" asked rathead, patting Benji on the chest.

"Good lungs," grunted a doghead nearby.

"He should fetch a good price on the slave market. Wouldn't you agree?" rathead said.

"Eggscuse! Eggscuse! Can't you see we're eggstremely busy."

"Good price, partner," grunted doghead.

"Partner!" exclaimed rathead. "No partners needed here. He's mine."

"Wrong, friend" a voice bellowed. "He's mine!"

It was Vitch, towering over the Mishmashan. "Now let him go," he commanded.

Rathead released Benji who promptly kicked him, making him wince.

"Vitch, fancy meeting you here" said doghead, forcing a smile. "Your son?" he asked. "A charming boy. We were just saying what a lovely sweet child he was. Is, I mean. Weren't we, Mashans?"

"Lovely child," growled lionhead.

"Cherub," grunted bearhead.

"We have been watching you, Vitch," said doghead. "And your son. We may have something you want."

"What is that?"

"Information."

"What information?"

"We know why you're here, don't we, Mashans?" His companions nodded solemnly.

"I just told you not 10 minutes ago I was looking for Arry," said Vitch.

"True. But Arry is not the one you want," bearhead spoke up. "In fact he never was. He's only doing a job. Selling those strange boxes your son found to someone of great repute. Someone who very much wants to – "

Before bearhead could go any further a squad of Rattatat soldiers burst into the garden firing guns. Yellow stun rays crisscrossed the area hitting just about everyone. There was bedlam. Benji ducked under a table.

As the noise of the battle died down Benji was able to make out the Mishmashans slumped unconscious on their chairs. Vitch was lying face down over a table.

"How's Vitch?" asked Seya climbing onto Benji's lap under the table.

"He's coming round," said Benji, noticing Vitch beginning to stir.

One of the soldiers stepped into the middle of the groaning bodies piled everywhere and began barking commands.

"My name is Jarv," he said in a cold hard voice, scanning the tables with gunmetal gray eyes. "I seek a boy," he announced, "a New Earthling. I know he is here. Has anyone anything to say, while I am still in a good mood?"

Everyone had now almost fully recovered from the stun rays.

Sorry Zeydeh, Benji thought from his hiding place under the table. I gave it my best, but now, the first chance I get I'm outa here. Whoever took your bag can keep it.

Just then, the commander signalled to his soldiers. They cocked their guns and took a more threatening stance.

"Nobody has been seriously hurt...yet," said Jarv, addressing them. "The boy will not be harmed, but my mood, I think, is beginning to change."

He began walking slowly through the square accompanied by three other soldiers. He paused at the Eggis' table. Without warning he brought down his mailed fist and smashed the table in two.

"Stop it, stop it," one of the Eggis cried out, panic-stricken. "I mustn't be eggcited. I have a bad heart. There was a boy here. Eggstremely rude too."

"And where did he go?"

"Over there," said the Eggi, pointing in Benji's direction.

Benji tried to make a break for it, but it was hopeless. One of the soldiers caught him before he travelled five steps. He was about to protest when something cold and painful touched the base of his neck. He wanted to cry out but before he could open his mouth he was in a deep, deep sleep.

He dreamed he was being stuffed into a blue bag that had the word Benji, written in Hebrew, embroidered on it.

Chapter 5
Zozabahl The Mutant

Benji awoke to find himself lying on a bed in a large room without doors or windows. A narrow air vent ran along the ceiling. Apart from the bed there was just a stool, a small table and a couple of chairs.

A thousand questions were hammering his brain but he couldn't answer a single one. Where was he? Why had they, whoever "they" were, been looking for him? And what was so valuable about his grandfather's tefillin that people or aliens would want to steal them?

Benji looked down at the tape around his finger. "Just snap your fingers," Vitch had told him. Would it work?

Before he had a chance to find out he heard a

click and a panel in the wall slid open.

A small figure walked in. It had green hair and a half-black half-white face. Benji realized it was a boy about his own age.

"My name is Piedo," said the boy, flatly. "Follow me."

"Where are we?" asked Benji, but the boy didn't reply.

It was a long walk, through dark halls and long corridors.

"In here," said Piedo, pointing to a simulated crusader castle door.

"Wow," gasped Benji, admiring its massive size.

Piedo lifted an iron door knocker and banged three times. Then he stepped back.

A hatch behind a metal grill opened and a beak-nosed face appeared.

"Who comes here?" asked the face loudly in a high-pitched nasal voice.

Benji looked around for Piedo, assuming he would reply, but he was no longer there.

"Psst," said the face, to get Benji's attention. "What's your name, boy?"

"Benji."

"Full name," hissed beaknose.

"Benji Kohen."

"Wait until I make my report," said beaknose loudly, closing the hatch.

Moments later the door creaked open and beaknose beckoned to Benji. "Come inside and don't speak until I say so."

He entered an enormous hall. There was a blood-red carpet stretched along its entire floor. At the far end was a large figure sitting on what looked like a throne. They walked slowly, beaknose wheezing as he went.

Finally, beaknose paused and bowed low.

"Whatever you do," he whispered to Benji as he straightened, "don't upset Zozabahl."

The name Zozabahl meant nothing to Benji, and all he could see was a fat face staring at him through evil green eyes. Zozabahl had one massive hand attached to the right side of his bloated body. On his left side were short, useless fingers that wiggled from what should have been his arm socket. The fingers on his right hand were fat and gnarled looking. The index finger, in particular, had the longest red nail Benji had ever seen.

"So you finally found the little monster," Zozabahl bellowed.

Benji heard a crack as beaknose snapped his bones to attention. "Yes sir!" Beaknose shoved Benji closer to Zozabahl.

"Don't push me, okay," said Benji, turning on him angrily.

"A boy with spirit," beamed Zozabahl, his green eyes expanding. "How refreshing. Come a little closer, Benji Kohen."

Benji climbed up one step. He dreaded being touched by this mutant.

"What do you want from me?" he asked. "I don't know anything."

"But I know everything about you, Benji Kohen," Zozabahl sneered. "Even about your grandfather and his sacred bag."

"Then you know that my grandfather gave me the bag to watch and that all I'm supposed to do is deliver it to him on Passover. That's all. So, why did you kidnap me and what am I doing here?"

Benji was angry. At that moment he would gladly have given this monster the bag, if he had had it. He was sick and tired of all the intrigue and suspicion. Had he known what was going to happen he would have let the police handle it from the start. How he wished for the police now.

"It's simple, Benji Kohen," continued Zozabahl. "There is something in that bag which is very important to me, something I have been looking for, for quite some time, something which you may be able to help me recover." He smiled a toothless grin. "You would help me if you could, Benji Kohen, wouldn't you?" he asked.

"Maybe," Benji carefully answered. "Why don't you tell me what you want of me?"

"Indeed," Zozabahl said, "why not." Turning to beaknose he commanded. "Bring me the bag!"

Beaknose scurried away. Within moments he

returned with the bag.

"The tefillin!" Benji gasped. "You have them!"

Zozabahl asked him, "Is this what your grandfather asked you to bring?"

"Yes," said Benji, excited.

"Do you know why he wants them?"

"He never said. He just told me to bring them for Pesach. I mean Passover."

"And did he tell you what he was going to do with them?"

"I said I don't know. Maybe they're so old he wants to bury them. Jews do that with religious stuff that gets old and worn." Old and worn stuff like you, he thought to himself.

"And where will he bury them?"

"I just said I think he may bury them," Benji reminded his interrogator.

"Well then where do you *think* he will bury them," yelled Zozabahl, hardly able to control his temper now.

"New Jerusalem, of course," murmured Benji, starting to be afraid again.

"Fine. Now we're getting somewhere. Did you ever look inside the bag?" asked Zozabahl.

"Once or twice I guess," mumbled Benji, wondering when the questions would end.

"Open it," ordered Zozabahl.

Benji unzipped the bag. Inside were two little black boxes on slightly larger bases with leather straps wound tight against the sides. They looked very old and very fragile.

Zozabahl handed Benji a piece of paper. "We had the contents of the boxes analyzed. Here is what it says."

Benji squinted, trying hard to make out the small handwritten characters.

"Well? Well?" shouted Zozabahl, unaccustomed to being kept waiting. "What is it boy?"

"It looks like Hebrew."

"Sooo you can read it can you?" Zozabahl smiled.

"No, I can't," said Benji flatly.

"Of course you can," insisted Zozabahl. "You're Jewish aren't you?"

"It's too small," said Benji almost sadly, "and it has no vowels."

"No vowels. Of course!" exclaimed Zozabahl. "It's coded. As I expected. Your zeydeh could read it though, couldn't he?"

"Maybe," answered Benji.

"Of course he can!" Zozabahl asserted. "And so can you! Read them. Now! We have use for these scrolls!"

"You want to use the tefillin?" Benji asked, trying to change the subject. "But you're not even Jewish!" he told him.

Zozabahl was taken aback by Benji's remark. He decided to pursue this new line of discussion.

Maybe the boy knew more than he thought. "What does being Jewish have to do with it?" he asked.

"Well, some Jews wear tefillin during their morning prayers."

"Have you ever asked yourself why?" Zozabahl interrupted.

"Uh, I suppose it's part of our tradition. I'll probably do the same when I grow older. So what?"

Actually, Benji had never given any real thought to wearing tefillin before. It all seemed so old fashioned. But now, he was beginning to wonder. Perhaps there was something to being part of a tradition that went back thousands of years. He would have to talk to Vitch or his zeydeh about this, when, and if he ever got away.

"I think it's more than just tradition, Benji Kohen," Zozabahl insisted. "As I'll soon show you, I think it is because of the power, because of the secret within the scrolls. The secret of the universe."

"Secret of the universe! What? Are you crazy!" Benji cried. He was tired of this mutant expecting him to know a secret that no one had ever told him.

What is it about my zeydeh's tefillin that drives everyone crazy? he said to himself. If I don't find out soon I'll go crazy myself!

"Listen, Mr. Zozabahl, this is just an old pair of tefillin. There are no secrets of the universe on its parchment. There are only prayers. I'm sorry I

Zozabahl handed Benji a piece of paper.

can't translate those prayers for you, but I was never a very good Hebrew School student. For that I'm doubly sorry. But that's the truth. The Hebrew words on the scrolls are no secret except to people who can't read Hebrew!"

"Well then you won't mind translating them for me," Zozabahl told him.

"Look, you don't seem to understand," Benji tried again to explain. "I can't translate the words because I really don't know what they mean. I only have an elementary Hebrew School education. I barely know enough words to fill one page of a holowriter. The words in the tefillin are from the Bible. Old Hebrew. The oldest. I don't know the language. I repeat, I DON'T KNOW THE LAN-GUAGE. You can torture me or threaten to kill me, but I still can't help you."

"Leave him to me, sir," beaknose said. "I will teach him to honor your commands."

But Zozabahl was beginning to believe Benji.

"Well, if you don't know anything about the parchment, then I really don't have any use for you," Zozabahl announced.

"Kill him," he ordered.

Chapter 6

Heads Begin To Roll

It never dawned on Benji that the fat mutant would actually kill him. "But I know someone who can read the scrolls," he quickly offered.

"Who?" Zozabahl asked.

"Vitch, the Jew who was with me when you kidnapped me. He belongs to some sort of group called HASHEM. Maybe he knows about your secret."

"How do I find this Vitch?"

"Easy, I just rub my finger here." He held out the finger with tape and began rubbing. Suddenly a voice was heard.

"Is that you, kid?" Talmon said.

"Yes, it's me," Benji responded. "I need Vitch."

"Vitch is right here, kid. What's happening?

Where are you?"

"He is with me!" boomed Zozabahl. "And he will be in the next world very soon if this fellow Vitch does not come here right now to translate these scrolls."

"I am Vitch," Vitch said, his voice very serious. "Tell me where you are and I will come at once. Just don't harm the boy."

"I am Zozabahl the magnificent," boomed the mutant.

"I know you Zozabahl!" Talmon suddenly interrupted. "Zozabahl the torturer! Zozabahl the putrid! Touch that boy and you'll find out first hand what the next world is all about."

"Ah, so it is you, Talmon," Zozabahl said, enjoying himself immensely. "I thought your voice sounded familiar. Then I suppose you already know where I am located. After all you were a guest of mine once before," he smirked.

"I still have the scars to remind me," Talmon spat. "Kid, hang in there, we're on our way."

"Don't worry boychick, Mayven and I will get you out of this. In less time than it takes to kasher a chicken," Vitch added, signing off.

"And now, Benji Kohen," Zozabahl leered as he turned to his captive, "while we are waiting for your friends let's have some entertainment."

He waved his hand and Piedo entered carrying a large black box on a silver tray.

"Well, don't just stand there, Piedo, put the platter on the floor," said Zozabahl, sharply. "Where the boy can see. Yes," he grinned, his mouth curving into a sinister smile, his green eyes glinting. "Where the boy can see."

Piedo obediently placed the tray down on the top step, just in front of Benji.

Zozabahl chuckled. "This is the part I like best," he said, pointing his long, red fingernail at the box.

Benji heard a ting and the box opened. For a moment, his mind rebelled against what his eyes saw. He shut them tight, hoping the things in the box would go away, but when he opened his eyes again they were still there. Three heads lined up neatly in a row: rathead, lionhead, and a lizard head. Benji realized that the last head must have belonged to the alien who originally stole the tefillin bag.

"If I get my hands on Arry Abadan, I'll add his ugly head to these," said Zozabahl dryly. "He tried to cheat me, you know. He tried to keep the scrolls for himself, but as you see I have them now."

Benji gulped. He still couldn't get over the fact that only a short time ago he had spoken to the two Mishmashans.

Zozabahl leaned towards Benji and told him in a quiet, confidential manner. "I don't like liars. People should always keep their promises wouldn't you agree?" Then, gazing beyond the boy, at the assorted heads on the columns along the wall, he added, "These three will make a splendid addition to my decor. As a matter of fact there's only one head that would be nicer on a pedestal than these...." He trailed off, staring at Benji and grinning.

"You won't cheat me will you, Benji Kohen?"

Benji finally found his voice. "But why did you kill the Mishmashans," he said, pointing at the two heads. "They didn't know much."

"But that's exactly why they had to be eliminated. They did not know enough. Unlike you Benji Kohen. You know enough to get me what I want, don't you my dear boy?"

"I-I th-think so," Benji stuttered. I hope so, he said to himself. "But tell me, how do you know there is such great power in the scrolls?" Benji asked, playing for time. "Maybe if I had more information I could help you discover the answers you need before Vitch comes. We may not even need him to read the scrolls. After all the scrolls were in my family for generations."

"That's true," Zozabahl nodded, thinking that it wouldn't hurt to show Benji how much he, Zozabahl, already knew about the secret of the scrolls. "But when you see my little presentation you may feel I have far more knowledge about the scrolls than either you or your ancestors."

Once again, he pointed his index finger, but this

time the entire wall on the right side of the hall lit up. Suddenly Arry Abadan, his donkey head grinning, appeared in holographic life, standing on a pile of rocks with a spade in his hand, speaking to the camera.

"I have recently unearthed a group of ancient stones that were buried in the tomb of King Psachatarta II, ruler of Midian and parts of Mesopotamia." He held up a stone tablet about the size of a large plate. "Our experts have been able to decipher most of this stone. It says as follows: 'These are the words that I, Sunmoon, god of all gods, command you. Take heed of the children of Israel for they hold the secret of the universe. Take heed of their power lest they destroy you. Beware their ornaments; that which they place between their eyes and on their hands.'

"So you see, Zozabahl," Arry continued, "there is some secret in the ornaments, the bag that the Kohen boy has with him."

Then the screen went blank.

"I don't understand," Benji said, "you can't believe that the scrolls in my grandfather's bag are thousands of years old. Certainly no one in my family knows about this ancient message from some make-believe god!"

"I suggest," Zozabahl advised, "you continue to watch the screen."

The wall erupted in light again. It seemed so

realistic Benji almost thought he was back at the spaceport. Then he saw himself arguing with his sister.

"The way you hold onto it anyone would think you found the secret of the universe."

"Maybe it is the secret of the universe."

"Saturn's rings! What are you talking about?"

"Have you seen what's inside?"

"I don't have to."

"They are very, very old."

"Benji, our zeydeh is very, very old. That's another secret of the universe I suppose."

The screen went blank again.

"Naturally," Zozabahl confided, "we had already known about the scrolls and your mission weeks earlier. But this confirmed what some had suspected, and I had known, since that thief Abadan uncovered the tablets. These scrolls are my destiny! They will give me the power of the ancients, the power of the universe!"

At last, Benji understood Zozabahl. This mutant actually believed all that voodoo about the Jews having the secret of the universe. Well, if there was a secret, he thought to himself, does Zozabahl really think the Jewish people would entrust it to a ten-year-old boy!

This is all a terrible mistake! he wanted to shout. But Benji knew that if he did so his head would be on a pillar in a matter of seconds.

Chapter 7
Run For Your Life!

"What about Abadan?" Benji asked, curious as to what part this mystery Mishmashan played. "What did he do to you?"

"It is not what he did," Zozabahl hissed, "it is what he did not do. Instead of bringing me the tablets and the scrolls, he decided to use their power for himself. Fortunately, my spies managed to steal the scrolls and return them here.

"Their heads are on those pillars," he said, pointing to two alien heads not far from Benji. "It is not wise to trust spies...even your own spies," he laughed.

Suddenly it was clear to Benji. He would be dead whether he helped translate the scrolls or not. He had nothing to lose.

In a burst of speed, Benji snatched the tefillin and began to run. Zigzagging down the aisle he deliberately banged into the columns, toppling the heads. He had no idea where he was going, but he didn't care.

Sirens blared. Stun rays seared the air in all directions. Zozabahl's men were chasing him. And they were close. He could hear their labored breathing.

Clearing the end of the aisle he turned sharply to the left and plunged into the darkness. He was in a maze which seemed to have no end. All Benji could see were shapeless lumps as he ran. Were they alive? Were they statues? More heads on pedestals? He wasn't going round in circles was he? He glanced over his shoulder. Black forms everywhere.

After a long time groping in the darkness and weaving in and out of corridors, he had to rest. Dropping to the floor he paused and listened. No sounds. But he wasn't taking anything for granted. He snapped his fingers, rubbing the transmitter. "Mayven, Vitch, Seya," he whispered, burying his mouth into the palm of his hand. "It's me, Benji. I've got the tefillin. I don't know where I am but you've got to help me. Maybe you could beam me out of here. Maybe...."

"The scrambler nullifies all unauthorized signals," said a voice in the darkness. "Whoever you're calling can't hear you."

It was Piedo. Then, as if from nowhere, Benji felt a ray gun against his head.

"It's all over," Piedo said.

In the darkness Benji saw his short ten years rewinding before his eyes. "Please," he pleaded, angry and afraid at the same time.

Before he could say anything more, another voice spoke.

"Drop the gun, Piedo." The boy instantly did as he was told.

"Now get against the wall. You, Benji, we have no time to lose. Take this monkey's gun," the voice commanded. Benji picked up the gun.

"I'm Arry Abadan," the voice said as they entered a partially lit hall. Sure enough the body next to Benji had the head of a donkey.

"What are you doing here?" asked Benji, running hard to keep up with the Mishmashan.

"I'm here to see to it that the secret of the universe stays out of the hands of Zozabahl. I switched bags before Zozabahl stole the scrolls from me. The bag you're holding is just a rather unique clone copy. The real bag is safely hidden. So don't worry."

"Huh?" Benji said, "Who cares about the bag. It's the tefillin that are important."

"You don't have to kid me, boy," Abadan smiled, making a turn into what looked like a dead end. "Remember, I read those stone tablets."

Benji decided now wasn't the time to try and make a point. But he was getting more confused all the time.

"This is the tricky part," Abadan told him, staring at the wall.

"What are you looking for?"

"A tiny lever."

Benji put the tefillin down to help Abadan find the lever. After a few moments, his hand touched something. He heard a click and the wall slid open, revealing a cave. Shouts and screams could be heard coming from behind them. Benji grabbed the tefillin but they seemed glued to the ground.

Abadan saw him tugging desperately. "It's the force field," he said from the other side of the opening. "They've activated all the fields. Leave the bag! If we don't escape now they'll kill us for sure."

Just then two of Zozabahl's guards came into view. They fired, but when the rays touched the field they scattered, bouncing all over the corridor. The next guards came and rushed the field. At first the weakened field looked like it might let them through but then it bounced them backward onto the floor.

"Come on," Arry yelled, "the field is disintegrating, we've got to move, NOW!" Without waiting for a reply he grabbed Benji and pulled him away from the tefillin. Then he pushed him into the cave. Benji began to run, but after a few moments he realized he was all alone. Without thinking, he turned and began racing back to help Arry.

"Keep moving," shouted the Mishmashan, almost running into him. "The field is down! They're coming through!"

Benji turned again and put on a last burst of speed as he flew out of the tunnel.

"AYIEE!" he shouted, as he realized he was actually flying. The tunnel had ended in a ten-foot drop. Benji, arms flailing wildly, fell to the ground, exhausted. Arry shot out of the tunnel and landed hard beside him, his donkey face grimacing with pain.

"No time to rest now," warned Arry, picking himself up. "They'll be coming through the cave any minute. Let's move!"

He dragged Benji onto his feet and they began running again. Then Benji saw it. A town. People. At last, they would be safe.

He would have laughed for joy, except that he suddenly realized his pain and suffering had all been for nothing.

The tefillin bag was gone.

*"Leave the bag! If we don't escape now
they'll kill us for sure."*

Chapter 8
Droids Attack

Breathless, the pair entered the town. Benji turned to ask Arry about the next part of his plan, but the Mishmashan had disappeared. He searched frantically but unsuccessfully for the donkeyhead.

Carefully, Benji touched the gun he still had in his pocket. Looking around he began to feel very out-of-place. He was the only human in a busy marketplace filled with alien forms.

Suddenly he felt a heavy hand on his shoulder. Without thinking, he pulled out his gun.

"Don't shoot, kid, or I won't be able to join you for Passover," said Talmon, smiling down at him. Before Benji could recover from his shock, Talmon continued, "Vitch is waiting for us at the far parking lot, past all these stalls."

Benji wanted to hug Talmon, and beg him to take him home. But before he could say anything a familiar voice hissed, "Talmon, three soldiers. Front right. They are circling in order to shoot the boy." It was Seya, and the fur on her back was standing straight up.

Talmon whipped around and fired. The first soldier was killed instantly. The second lost his hand. He couldn't find the third. Without warning, a laser beam sizzled past, singeing Talmon's ear and Seya's head. Talmon fired back and the soldier fell.

"Behind you," warned Seya.

A droid was closing in. Talmon fired but the rays skimmed off its armor plate. The droid drew out a long wand and charged. Talmon fired again and again, point blank, but the rays just bounced away and the droid kept on coming.

Talmon side-stepped the first thrust of the wand and yelled to Benji to run but Benji was frozen in place. The droid wrapped one of its tentacles around Talmon's feet and flipped him over. Talmon was dazed. With a triumphant snarl the droid raised its wand for the final blow. But Benji suddenly sprang into action. He leaped on the spiny back of the droid throwing him off balance. That was all Talmon needed. He took out his Azurian knife and slashed at the droid just under its helmet. Wordlessly, the droid dropped to the ground, twitched, and ceased functioning. But, as Talmon picked himself up another droid rushed him, wand raised. Before Talmon could move out of the way a laser beam seared the droid's head and it too collapsed.

"With droids, it's not what you say, but where you say it."

It was Arry Abadan.

Pulling Talmon to his feet he asked, jokingly, "Drunk again, Talmon?"

Shoving and elbowing their way out of the crowded market they joined the mad rush to the parking lot where ships were zooming off in all directions.

"Talmon," warned Seya, jumping onto his shoulder, "both ends."

A troop of droids and soldiers was converging upon them.

"Too many," Talmon yelled, pulling Benji behind a parked shuttle. "We've got to make a run for it," he told him.

"Start the engine, Vitch," said Talmon, rubbing his fingers. "We're coming right to you so leave the hatch open. It wouldn't hurt if you could give us a little protection either."

"Just get close enough and we'll blast them those mishumids back to Gehennom!" Vitch told him.

At the count, everyone ran. Once again, Benji found himself in the air as Talmon scooped him up and held him in a sprinter's grasp. There were so many vehicles in the parking lot the droids and soldiers couldn't get a clear shot. But neither could Vitch.

When they were within hailing distance of the spaceship, Talmon turned around. "Get into the ship," he commanded. "I'll cover you until Vitch starts firing. Go! Go! GO!"

Everyone moved toward the spaceship. Vitch started firing, keeping most of the droids and soldiers at bay. But there were too many of them. As Talmon fired, a ray found its mark and Talmon went down. He was hit in the shoulder.

Benji turned around and saw his friend fall. "Arry!" he screamed. "Look!"

Without missing a step Arry turned around and, firing, ran back to get Talmon. Benji, following Arry's lead, began firing also but before long the gun proved too heavy for him to hold. They reached Talmon and tried to drag him to safety. The droids saw their chance and charged, their tentacles whipping through the air. The closest droid pointed his wand directly at Benji.

Benji closed his eyes...and fainted.

Chapter 9
Plenty Of Tzorris

Benji woke up with a start as he heard Vitch say, "Don't worry, Mayven has ringed you in a protective force field." The strip on his hand was warm. "I'll have you aboard for mincha," Vitch assured him. The spaceship was directly above them, spewing deadly bullets (a vestige from the old days no doubt) and causing havoc among the droids and soldiers. The bullets bounced off the droid's armor but they made such a racket that the aliens ran.

"Grab Talmon and get in here," Vitch told them as he landed only a few feet away. Benji, Arry, and even Seya pushed and pulled until they got Talmon into the open bay doors. With a sputter and a whoosh, the ship took off. Once aboard, they cleaned and bandaged Talmon's wound, and settled in.

Benji was depressed. To go through all this and then end up without his grandfather's tefillin was more than he could handle. He could take the yelling and lecturing he would get from his parents, and his sister, but how would he ever be able to face his grandfather again?

"What's the matter, boychick?" Vitch asked him. "Mayven and I can handle any tzorris you may have."

"What's tzorris?" Benji asked, more to take his mind off his problems than out of curiosity. There was very little he understood about Vitch. But somehow the old man made him feel comfortable, like his zeydeh.

"Just what it sounds like. A burning, terrible, itch that won't go away. A plague that seems to hover over your head. A bout of hiccups that keeps you from eating or drinking or sleeping. A –"

"Okay, I get the point. Yes, I have tzorris. A big one. What am I going to do when I have to face my zeydeh without the tefillin?"

"Look how nice the boy says the word 'zeydeh', Mayven," Vitch smiled, "he's a natural, a potential tzadik, one of the hidden 36 great ones."

"Stop torturing the boy," Arry said.

"What?" Vitch said, surprised.

"Why don't you tell him that I have the scrolls."

"You do?" Benji jumped up, turning to Arry.

"I was getting to it," Vitch assured him. "I just

wanted to see how the boy handled tzorris."

Benji was too excited to be angry at Vitch.

"Here are the scrolls," Arry offered, handing Benji the tefillin. "And they're in their original bag."

Just then Mayven announced that they would shortly be landing on Rattatat 5.

"Before I leave I have a small request," Arry said, examining the embroidered writing on the tefillin bag.

"Nu," said Vitch, as Talmon came into the room.

"Well," said Arry, "seeing as I saved the boy and the tefillin I feel I should get a little something for my trouble. Don't you agree?"

Vitch gave him a sour look. "How much?"

"Oh, not money," said Arry. "I was thinking more along the lines of a little memento."

"Okay, you old grave robber," said Talmon. "Spit it out."

"I want the bag," Arry declared.

"What!" said Benji. "Droids!" he shouted holding the tefillin tightly. "Why don't you just keep the clone copy?"

"I would, except that professionals like myself find it easy to detect even these near-perfect duplicates. I won't be able to get a tarnished golden for a clone copy. For the original, well, there are some collectors on Pramadan who would give their right nose for this bag."

"What about the secret of the universe? Aren't you interested in the scrolls themselves?" Benji asked, curious as to why Arry was asking for only half the pie.

"Oh that, well, I don't really believe those ancient gods. The truth is I sort of embellished a bit on what the stones said. Oh, there was mention of the children of Israel all right, but only a slight, unintelligible word or two about symbols and ornaments and stuff like that. Anyway, I figured it was a good way to get a few goldens from that fool Zozabahl. If he hadn't been so greedy he would probably have your bag and the scrolls right now. But fair is fair. He tried to dork me, so I dorked him first."

Benji had to smile. But that didn't mean he was going to part with the tefillin, or the bag.

"Kid, he has a point." Talmon said. "He's in it for the goldens, but he did save you and me. We owe him."

Horrified, Benji couldn't believe Talmon. "No! After all I've gone through I can't let him just take it —"

Suddenly a furry flash snatched the bag in its teeth and scurried out of reach beneath the seats.

"Seya," said Benji, "you stay there until Arry's gone, okay."

"That's not why she took it, kid," said Talmon.

"Benji," said Vitch, "as a member of HASHEM I

can tell you that what your zeydeh really wants are the tefillin. The bag is unimportant."

"Not you too," said Benji turning to Vitch. He could not believe another Jew, a religious Jew, would talk like that.

"It's not yours to trade," he insisted. "I'm going to report you, both of you," he said bitterly. Everyone looked at him. He was outnumbered, in more ways than one.

With tears in his eyes, and realizing there was nothing else he could do, Benji reluctantly agreed.

"They're right," he finally admitted, staring at the donkeyhead. "You saved my life and I'm sure my zeydeh would want you to have his bag. And, if my friends say it is okay, then I trust them," he sighed, looking from Talmon to Vitch. "But I hope I never see you again," he blurted out to Arry.

Talmon put a comforting hand on Benji, but Benji shrugged it off. Then he handed the boy a note. Benji recognized his zeydeh's scrawl. It read:

Talmon works for me. Trust him, Benji. Your loving zeydeh, Abraham Kohen.

"Why didn't you give me this in the beginning," Benji sniffled, wiping away some tears.

"Well, kid," Talmon smiled, "I've learned the hard way that the only road to trust is through the mountains of experience. If you couldn't trust me because of me, a note wouldn't help much."

For the first time Benji realized that Talmon had been watching over him from the moment he left the spaceport. He looked up at Talmon, smiled, and gave his friend a big hug.

In the background, he heard Mayven announcing, "Mincha! Mincha in ten minutes!"

Chapter 10
The Secret Of The Universe

They were all seated at the Passover table. Talmon looked uncomfortable in holiday clothes, Vitch wore a flowing white robe, Seya sat on a cushion, and Benji had a place of honor next to his grandfather. Benji's parents and his sister sat on his other side.

"Benji," his grandfather began, "you are the youngest. Please recite the traditional 'Ma Nishtana' from the Haggadah." Then, as though reconsidering his request he added, "Perhaps before you do, you can share with us your personal feelings about tonight?"

Benji stood up, looking at the smiling faces around him. "Zeydeh, I think I understand much more about our people's flight from slavery to freedom than I ever did before. I think I realize what it means to be chased and persecuted for no real reason. I even think I understand what the Egyptians must have felt when the Plague of Darkness settled over them and they didn't know what was happening to them. "Then, looking at Vitch, he added, "And I definitely know the meaning of tzorris!"

They all laughed.

"Ah, Reb Avraham, your grandson is a tzadik, a tzadik," Vitch beamed.

After a moment, Talmon asked the question on everyone's mind. "Could you tell us, Rabbi, what was so special about this tefillin?"

Pointing to the tefillin sitting on the mantlepiece, Zeydeh explained.

"I know you all think that Zozabahl was crazy, and that Arry Abadan was just a gonif. I suppose in a sense you are right."

"They thought your tefillin held the secrets of the universe. Isn't that crazy?" Benji laughed.

"Well, perhaps," his zeydeh replied. "Yet the fact remains that Zozabahl and Abadan were not entirely wrong."

Everyone gasped.

"You mean to tell us, Rabbi," said Talmon, "that they do conceal a secret message?"

"Zeydeh, you must be kidding" Esti said, only half sure herself.

"Since Earth was destroyed at the turn of the

They were all seated at the Passover table.

21st century," Zeydeh continued, "we Jews have
waited to return to Earth Prime to rediscover our
history." He paused and dramatically lowered his
voice. "Now I can disclose that for centuries this
family has been the guardian of a coded message
that for us holds great secrets. The message tells us
where to find the hidden treasures of our Temple
in Old Jerusalem."

"But why put such an important piece of information on parchment," said Benji, starting to get
confused again. "It crumbles," he wisely noted.

"It's not on the parchment, Benji," Zeydeh confided, opening the bag and taking out the black
boxes. "It's in the thread used to sew and seal the
boxes. It's a special silicon. On it are the histories of
the Kohen family, and thousands of other families
scattered across the galaxy. It contains information
concerning our heritage and where to find hundreds of Torah scrolls – the real secret to our survival – which were hidden before the War.

"The tefillin themselves," Zeydeh said, picking
them up, "were not meant for prayer. They were
designed only to look like the real thing, to fool
would-be gonifs like Zozabahl and Abadan. They
look old, but that's because we use a special process
to give them an ancient smell and feel."

"Copy cloning!" declared Benji.

"Why yes," his grandfather said, amazed at
Benji's knowledge.

"And everything was copy cloned?" Benji asked.

"Everything, except the silicon thread of course," his grandfather admitted.

"Even the bag?" Benji persisted.

"Certainly."

"Great!" Benji shouted, and then began to laugh. Everyone except Zeydeh joined the laughter.

"It looks like Arry was not much of a mayven himself," Vitch added.

"I don't understand what is so funny," Zeydeh said. "But I'm sure you'll tell me during the Seder. Right now, Reb Vitch," he said, presenting him with the tefillin, "our job is almost complete."

"Why are you giving the tefillin to him?" asked Esti.

"Vitch is the head of HASHEM, that stands for Hassidus, Holiness, and Emunah, the three pillars upon which the future of Judaism rests. He is in charge of rebuilding Old Jerusalem."

Then Zeydeh turned to his grandson. "And now Benji, you may give us the traditional version of why this night is different from all other nights."

Benji cleared his throat, and began to sing.

Cholent

by Peter Syle

CHOLENT – (chŭ-lent) *n.* **1.** a native of the planet Yapzug. Cholents emit toxic shmertz gas as a by-product of their breathing. Their gaseous blue bean bubble-bursts are considered deadly to all nosed species. **2.** a bean-based food served by Jews on their Sabbath and cooked for approximately 24 hours.

Excerpt from: *Webster's Thirty-Fifth Intergalactic Dictionary, Earth Prime Edition*

Contents

Chapter 1
Well Done!

"Sir, we've spotted one," reported the leader of the search-and-destroy unit.

Data links sent the new flow of information into the large hall that served as the control center of the needle-nosed destroyer.

"It's an adult with deep brown colorations, bubbles bursting at a fantastic rate. Strange, it doesn't even see us, yet our filters are starting to turn gray. We can't recycle fast enough."

There was a pause. Then, it seemed, a thousand mouths spoke at once.

"Captain, we're in trouble.... The filters.... We can't.... I repeat, we're in trouble!"

Without warning, ear-splitting screams ripped through the air. But before the captain on con deck could react, the crazed sounds of retching and heaving that had echoed through the hall, stopped.

Everyone knew that the members of the search-and-destroy unit were all dead.

The First Officer stared straight at the captain. He saw a touch of fear hidden deep within the other's wide yellow eyes. But in a moment that fear vanished.

"Battle stations, everyone," the captain shouted, putting on his privispeak, the beta-wave amplifier that put him in constant telepathy with every sector of the craft. "We have to find out what it's up to, and why it wasn't on Yapzug during the attack."

Turning to his First Webman, he commanded, "Prepare the web. Maximum force."

A flurry of activity signalled the beginning of webbing as the webmen took their stations.

"Helm, bring us up just over those ridges," the captain ordered, pointing to the wall of jagged hills visible from the holoview. "Not too high. We can't let it see us. When we're in position, begin webbing procedure."

As the ship began to rise, the lone cholent was completing a series of experiments. If the new mutated gas he was developing could be duplicated and cross-beamed to other cholents, then humanoids would no longer fear the inhabitants of Yapzug. With luck, his people would be permitted to trade with the entire galaxy, instead of being confined to the few non-nosed planets. Had he not been so involved in the results of his project the cholent's sensitive silica would certainly have warned him of the approach of the spaceship. But he had felt secure knowing that the huge wall directly behind him would serve as protection against any sneak attack.

Of course, he was not without personal protection. Every once in a while, he would send bursts of shmertz gas shooting out toward the hills in front of him. It was this gas that had eliminated the search-and-destroy unit hiding behind those hills.

As to his main warning system, he had tuned his extro-sensors to their lowest level, so he could devote all his energies to the project at hand.

It was a mistake he was about to pay for. Dearly.

"Strand one in place sir," a web runner announced.

"Strand two in place sir," echoed another.

"Triangular strand locked in sir," the First Webman reported. "We are ready to web."

"Web!" spat the captain, both mentally and verbally, as the ship jerked slightly from the tremendous energy being instantly transferred into the web pattern.

The cholent felt a sharp pain in his outer parts. Before long, the pain proved too great to ignore. He went into a defensive position, sending acid drops flying hundreds of feet. In rapid fire, bean bubbles began bursting. Deadly gases hissed out of these bubbles. Soon, a cloud of shmertz gas moved slowly along the moon's floor.

But it was too late. The web had sent its burning laserspears deep into the cholent's body. The pain was so great it shut down, no longer able to explode a single bean. It began to die.

As the web's suction rays carefully brought the cholent into the ship's specially designed antacid tanks the captain permitted himself a little smile. It spread from his first to his third and then his seventh set of lips. The tanks would keep the cholent alive long enough to take back to Earth Prime.

"Let's head back, gentlemen," the captain announced. "Well done," he complimented them, rapidly blinking four of his eyelids in a victory sign. "We've done it. We've captured one of them alive. Maybe now we'll finally know what makes cholent tick."

At the very word, *'cholent'*, most of the crew automatically held up half-a-dozen hands each, blocking most of the noses scattered around their heads.

Using their remaining hands, the multimorphosils applauded.

The cholent went into a defensive position sending acid drops flying hundreds of feet.

Chapter 2
The Last Cholent

The cholent lay in a heap. He reviewed within his being, word for word, everything he had told the Council. He chewed and re-chewed every syllable he had mind-linked to the Council members.

The cholent had been in a depressed state. His beans were terribly discolored and popping without any real rhythm. Yet beyond the hopelessness he had felt, lay a terrible, terrible rage. For the Council members' had told the cholent that his once proud and noble race had been brutally ripped out of the universe.

He knew why. As he knew that the Council members, almost all multimorphosils, were here only to witness their final, ultimate victory: the death of the last cholent.

He had agreed to mind-link with the Council, cross-species, because, despite his natural revulsion at such thought transfer, the cholent wanted to have his words recorded for all the worlds to remember.

He began by speaking simple truths.

"I suppose there will always be those who consider my race bizarre and dangerous," the cholent had said. "A kind of leftover from some practical cosmic joke that God saw fit to play on the universe, during the boring times between creations.

"Maybe it's true. Maybe to you I do look like a pile of simmering beans heaped 3 feet high and 4 feet wide and slightly overcooked. And of course, it's true that we cholents do burst bean bubbles, releasing deadly (to you) shmertz gas.

"But let me remind you, you did not create us, nor we you. Our bodies are ideal for our way of life, as yours are for yours. Remember too, it was your Federation that asked us to join them, asked us to help them in the Alpha Centurii Wars. And we, unfortunately, agreed.

"Then the deaths. Of course we had no way of knowing the effects of shmertz gas on your bodies. We had only met the earthlings, the single-nosed humans who were able to have limited contact with us. They learned from us, and we from them.

"Remember, you multimorphosils initiated contact with Yapzug. How could we have known your noses would be so sensitive, or so numerous? Just as we could not control our breathing, neither could you. As we breathed out, you breathed in, and died."

Then the cholent screamed his thoughts at them: "THIS WAS NOT OUR FAULT. WE DID NOT PLAN THIS. WE WERE ONLY BEING OUR-SELVES.

CHOLENT.

"And yet your weakness of nose made me and my kind outcasts. For you forced the Federation to forbid us the right to trade with the Intergalactic Worlds. You forced the nosed worlds to treat us as though we had the Dysentrian Plague. All this, after we helped you win your foolish wars.

"Now you have squeezed me into this chamber and forced me to mind-link with you, cross-species! For what? So you can kill me too? So you can fill this chamber with antacid dissolving me inch by inch until I die?

"And what do you gain? You will always be known as the ones who destroyed an entire race just because you could not stomach us. The universe will laugh at you, and hate you for having turned on beings who meant you no harm.

"For my part, my race is finished. Without pta-tors, our basic nutrient of life, I cannot bring any young cholents into existence. Without a new batch of cholents my race will become extinct, as is your wish.

"The curious thing is that we cholents had finally found a way to deal with you noseys. I was on our moon perfecting the first eggrot gas, a smelly, but not dangerous, bean gas. Our bean pods would have been able to produce this gas for hours at a time. With your filters you could have finally approached us, face-to-face, unafraid. But that is no longer important.

"Before you kill me, let me just repeat, for the record, what our Redbean Ambassador explained to you at the last United Galactic Assembly. There are over fifty planets in the Federation whose inhabitants don't have or need noses. We'd already agreed to work only through them. All contact with your species would have been limited as you saw fit. But even that was not enough. You insisted on treating us like garbage, like something to be chewed up and spat out. Ultimately, you invented excuses to try to destroy us. And you succeeded."

There was nothing else to say. Surprisingly, the Council decided not to destroy him. Instead they sent him into exile. He would have to wander through space forever. Nor was he permitted to land on any Federation planet, or trade his gases or acids for ptators. Without ptators he could not reproduce. Without ptators he was the last of his race. The last cholent from the planet Yapzug.

The Council thought they had solved their problem. But they did not understand the full power of cholent.

Chapter 3
The Multi And The Jew

"Captain, we've got alarms blaring all over the place but the screens don't show any sign of an attack," the First Officer barked, from a number of mouths. He was frantic as he looked at the maze of lights blinking wildly across his panel. Screeching sirens blasted his sensitive thirteenth ear.

Captain Velgrayd was human. And, as always, he was calm. He thought how much more pleasant life would be if Command Center didn't always stick him with the untried, inhuman, multimorphosils. How he hated these multis, with their multiple ears and multiple eyes and multiple noses and multiple everything, including row after row of disgusting teeth. Every time some little emergency occurred the multis would begin waving their extra arms all over the place doing more harm to the ship than any low level emergency ever could. But go tell Command Center that multis were a danger out here in deep space. Why, just the mention of it could cause another Tarlycon War.

Suddenly, despite the chaos, the captain smiled. He remembered a line from an old song he had heard as a child on Earth Prime.

The multi and the Jew,
There can never be too few.

"Give me some readings, Sasset," the captain snapped. "There must be some indication somewhere that we are under attack. Where's the damage?"

"On the B-3 quadrant of the ship, sir," another multi spoke up. "Right at the belly of the Starfarer, -sir."

Sasset realized at once that a fellow multi, of lower status, had spoken out of turn. He could not permit this to continue.

"My colleague, Sub-con Officer Zazzort, is correct sir," Sasset interrupted, placing himself between Zazzort and the captain. "However, I have discovered that the source of the attack is not from outside the Starfarer, sir. Not exactly that is."

Captain Velgrayd hated imprecision. He hated anything or anyone who was not clear in his thinking and his actions. So it was natural that he hate all multis who seemed to be forever thinking and

*The multis would begin waving their extra arms all over
the place doing more harm to the ship....*

re-thinking their decisions.

"Precision! First Officer," the captain shouted, "Precision, I tell you, or I'll rip every ear off your ugly face. Precisely where is the attack?"

"Precisely, sir," Sasset repeated, aware that the captain was not beyond carrying out such a threat. "The attack is coming from something attached to the ship, the mid-section of the ship. Sir."

"This is Victor speaking," the ship's computer announced to everyone in the control center. It used its deep male voice, the voice it preferred whenever the ship was in danger.

"We are being attacked by a high grade acid that is dissolving sections B-3, B-4, and B-5 of the ship. I have calculated that if this attack continues the ship will completely disintegrate in 3 days and 14 hours.

"However, please be warned that air-breathing life on the Starfarer will cease to exist in approximately 9 hours, unless the attacker is destroyed."

"What about the shields, Victor?" the captain asked.

"The shields are useless, Captain," the computer answered, "since the invader is already within the ship. Use of the shields would only draw it deeper into the ship's compartments and might actually damage the ship itself."

"What kind of being is this invader, Victor?" Velgrayd asked.

"Cholent." came the one-word answer.

Fear spread to every face in the control center. The captain, too, experienced a moment of disbelief. Like everyone else, he had been assured that all cholents had been burned to a crisp when the multis destroyed Yapzug.

Captain Velgrayd knew that the multis had been the ones who carried out the massacre on Yapzug. With their many noses, they were especially sensitive to the gaseous bubble-bursts that were the normal function of the cholents' breathing system.

Years earlier, at the Academy, the captain learned that there had always been an uneasy truce between the inhabitants of Yapzug and the nosey worlds. The cholents traded their high BTU gases and powerful acids for the ptators that grew throughout most of the Federation planets. Unfortunately, the land on Yapzug was so drenched with acid, it could no longer grow ptators. Yet without this common vegetable, cholents could not reproduce. So, the once proud beings of this small planet were forced to sell their gases and acids to other worlds in order to buy ptators.

It was these gases and acids that helped the Federation to win the Alpha Centurii Wars. But, just as the wars were winding down, a rumor began circulating across the galaxy.

Noseys were warned that the cholents had

begun eating meat! Since no nosey could protect itself from cholent gases for long, humanoids, especially multis, began to panic. They were sure the cholents would send wave after wave of their deadly gases to the unprotected nosey planets. When the gas clouds cleared, the cholents would begin their feast!

The multis decided they had to act fast. In a surprise raid, they blasted the inhabitants of Yapzug. They used titanium bombs to scorch the planet. Yapzug was a burned shell in a matter of hours. The one-sided battle was won so quickly because cholents had never perfected nor needed space missiles. Sizzling acid was the main defense used by cholents against their natural enemies on Yapzug, the flying beandragons and slimy forkfingers. The swirling gas-acid clouds that encircled Yapzug were considered sufficient to stop any military attack. No ship's oxygen system could handle the gases that surrounded the planet for long. Only robot-controlled spaceships could enter Yapzug's atmosphere. But robots were not permitted by Federation law to fire weapons that might harm any living thing.

That was why none of the crew members of the twenty-three spaceships that attacked Yapzug survived. The multis aboard their destroyers had known from the start that this was a suicide mission. Their deaths had been horrible, but their hatred of cholents was so ingrained that they were happy to die as martyrs.

The lone cholent that had survived his planet's destruction had been on Yapzug's moon testing the new, mutated strain of gas that some of his beans were emitting. He had just determined that the rotten egg smell these beans gave off was much less harmful to noseys than anything the cholents had ever produced. Yapzug would finally be able to live in harmony with its neighbors.

But, of course, by the time the cholent had isolated the DNA strain that produced this non-deadly gas, it was too late. Both for him and his planet.

Chapter 4

"Jews Eat Cholent?"

Victor," the captain commanded, switching his privispeak to a special frequency that only the ship's computer could receive. "I thought cholents were extinct."

"Clearly they are not," came Victor's dry reply. "Although this is the first attack by a cholent that I have cataloged in over 25 years."

"How do we get rid of it, Victor?" the captain snapped, watching the rest of the crew running from one set of instruments to another. New lights began flashing every few minutes and warning bells continued clanging.

"We have a limited antacid supply, Captain. We must pour it into the areas where the cholent has attached itself. In this way we may be able to neutralize its acid long enough to send in repair crews."

"A holding action then," remarked the captain, looking worried for the first time.

"Yes, Captain," Victor agreed, "but I would suggest trying to mind-link as well. We must find out more about this cholent. My sensors are already analyzing the special acids it is using to destroy the Starfarer. A team should also be sent to keep the cholent busy while I pour the antacid into the hold."

"We need volunteers," shouted the captain, removing his privispeak.

"I volunteer!" yelled one multi.

"Take me!" clamored another.

Dozens of mouths babbled simultaneously. They all wanted to volunteer. They all wanted the honor of what they knew would be a suicide mission.

But Captain Velgrayd was not paying attention to them. He was looking straight at one of his navigators, a human, clearly out of place among the multis.

"Nav Two," the captain said, pointing. "I understand your people have had quite a bit of experience with cholents. As a matter of fact didn't I hear that Jews actually eat cholents?"

The multis in the con tower showed signs of becoming physically sick.

"Only cholents that don't try to eat us first," the Nav Two jokingly answered. Neither the multis nor the captain thought much of his humor.

"My people use to eat something that looked similar to the...uh...cholent," he said much more seriously. "A long time ago," he added. "It's just a coincidence that in our mother tongue the name of that food also happened to be cholent.

"Quite honestly, Captain, I don't know any more about this alien than anyone else does. Less, in fact, since I've never even seen what a cholent looks like. That's because I missed the class on Interstellar Species at the Academy," he admitted. The captain continued to stare at him. Without knowing why, the Nav Two meekly added, "I was getting married at the time."

"Congratulations, Nav Two," the captain smiled, happy with himself for having succeeded in making the Jew so uncomfortable. "It looks like you'll get a chance to make up that class you missed in a real-life lab situation," he told his navigator.

The multis began to giggle.

"And thank you," the captain continued, "for volunteering. Now, suit up. There will be a squad of multis from A deck here in a moment."

Just then the con door opened and 15 multis entered. They formed a line and saluted.

"This is your commanding officer," he said, pointing to the Nav Two. The multis began to murmur. For them, being led on a suicide mission by a non-multi was an insult. Of course, the captain knew this. So did the Nav Two.

"I expect you to follow his orders precisely, just as you would mine," the captain explained. "Remember to use only your highest grade filters, and make sure you stick an air tube up every one of your ugly flopping nostrils."

"Yes sir," the multis responded with their first five mouths.

Still grumbling through the rest of their mouths, they followed the Nav Two out the door and toward the weapons quarters. Secretly, a number of multis were considering ways of making sure their commanding officer would be dead well before they attacked the cholent.

Shimshon Zuzstein was angry at himself. First, for being afraid of the captain and second, for letting the captain make a fool of him. Yet, for Navigator Second Grade (Nav Two) Shimshon Zuzstein, life had always been like this. Being picked for dangerous jobs was part of the price he had to pay for having been born Jewish. Being the butt of jokes and anti-semitic remarks was another part of that price.

Jew-hatred had reared its head, again, with the start of the Alpha Centurii Wars. The Jews were a small minority throughout the galaxy, but they were found on almost every humanoid planet. The ease with which they traded among themselves made the governments of many planets nervous. The Jews did not join the standard intergalactic organizations. They did not take advantage of many of the new freedoms that space travel offered. Many Jews dressed, ate, and even talked differently from what was considered the norm on most planets.

Yet, each world had its own Jewsies, the name the Federation planets called Jews. The Jewsies contributed more than their portion of the "Universal Tax" to the Federation. In return, they received SMI (Superior Merchant Interworld) passports which gave them an advantage over other interworld traders. More importantly, they were granted the right to practice their religion on every planet. This permitted them to worship their God even on planets where traders had to follow the religion of the host world.

All this, however, did not prevent the Federation from considering Jews as potential traitors when the Alpha Centurii Wars broke out. After all, there were Jews on Alpha Centurii, the enemy star cluster, too. And these Jews continued to keep contact with those on the Federation planets all during the wars. It was possible, many governments felt, that the Jews were sending messages to each other in the Jewsie language.

In order to protect themselves, the Federation planets developed a number of different methods to control their Jewish populations. Some planets kept round-the-clock watch on their Jews. They set up spy networks that worked within the Jewish population, trying to find traitors. Some planets created asteroid prisons where most of their Jews were sent until the wars were over. And some, like Earth Prime, drafted all Jews over 18 to fight Alpha Centurii. Drafting Jewsies was designed to show the other worlds that the government of Earth Prime trusted their Jews. Actually, however, it was their way of making sure the Jews remained loyal. After all, if the Jews were fighting for Earth Prime, they would hardly be able to betray their home planet.

Unfortunately, even after the Jews helped win the wars, Earth Prime, and many other worlds, continued drafting them. This, despite the fact that a draft was no longer needed, or used, on the rest of the population.

So much for trust.

"Are you there Nav Two?" the captain's voice blared through Shimshon's helmet. "What's going on?" he wanted to know.

"Sorry sir," Shimshon said, angry at himself, again, for apologizing all the time. "We're almost there, sir."

"Well, stay awake," warned the captain. "If you can freeze the cholent with nitrogen mogs, do so, even if it causes additional damage to the ship. One well-directed spray from the mog should put it out of action long enough for us to dunk it into the antacid tanks. But, don't let those martyr-mad multis convince you to attack the cholent unless you're sure you can freeze it, understood?"

"Understood, Captain," the Nav Two answered.

"And please be warned," Victor added, after the captain signed off, "you will have approximately 17 minutes from the time you enter the hold until your gas filters cease to function. Accomplish what you can and then retreat. At all costs, stay on the walls and ceiling so that the acid does not destroy your boots. I will line the walls with as much antacid as I can spare."

Shimshon was about to sign off when the computer suddenly continued.

"Since the captain has not informed you, please note that no one is to touch any broken bean shells. Most bean shells still have sufficient gas in them to seriously damage your filters. Furthermore, when you hear a bean burst lie flat against the wall and let the gas pass. Remember shmertz gas always flows downward even in 0 gravity. If you stay close to the ceiling you may be able to avoid the worst of it."

Shimshon wondered why the captain had not informed him of these dangers. Maybe he wasn't aware of them either....Or maybe....

"Okay," the captain cut in, "That's enough talk. Now go!"

Actually, the captain hated sending men, even

multis, on a suicide mission. But he had secret orders from Federation. All dangerous missions calling for volunteers were first to be filled by Jews and multis. The multis seemed to enjoy these kinds of missions. Suicide was a way of life with them; especially on their crowded planets.

But the Jews were different. They rarely volunteered. They rarely mingled. They made good, intelligent officers, but whenever two Jews met they would often revert to their native tongue, Habra. It made others uneasy. Especially Prime Earth veterans, like Captain Velgrayd. They didn't trust people who refused to change with the times.

For a moment, though, he felt sorry for the Nav Two. He knew that the chances of any of the men returning were very slim. Even if the cholent didn't attack them directly, its ordinary breathing would release more than enough gases to send the men to their deaths.

But Captain Velgrayd had little time for pity. He had the rest of the ship to worry about while Victor was busy analyzing the cholent's gases. The captain hoped that his computer could create some antidote. Better yet, a way to stop the cholent's breathing, so that the next wave of multis would be able to get closer and destroy it. A lot depended on the Jew, Zuzstein, slowing the cholent down – quickly.

Before all the beings on the Starfarer died.

Chapter 5

Blue Bean Bubble-bursts

Minutes passed. Reports kept coming in of additional areas of the ship dissolving. The captain knew that the damage to the ship would soon reach a point where repair would be impossible. His privispeak was receiving the grim statistics that indicated how many of the ship's crew were dead. It was not the acid that killed most of them. The acid could only spread slowly and affected the ship more than the crew. But the gases were invading the ship's air filters, reaching every level. He knew that at this very minute dozens of his crew were dying as the cholent's gases spread onward. Soon, only the control center with its independent filter system would be able to support life.

And even then they would only have an additional 3-4 hours.

"Are the air filters still holding?" thought the captain, turning his privispeak to Victor's private code.

"Yes Captain." Victor sent his words directly into the captain's brain. "But, unfortunately, the gases are seeping to the other levels through the many shafts and tunnels within the ship. If we try to seal --"

Suddenly, wild screams could be heard blaring out of the speakers in the control center.

"Captain, the acid..." yelled a multi. "Captain, the acid..." echoed another of the same multi's mouths. "It's eating through my suit....It's eating through my suit....It's eating...ahhhhhhh!"

"There isn't enough antacid, sir," shouted Shimshon over the cries of his men, "and we can't get close enough to fire a nitrogen mog. It's seen us, sir, and it's bursting bubbles at an amazing rate. We're trying to keep above the gases.

"The problem, Captain," he continued, signaling what men he had left to spread out, "is that the cholent is able to spray its acid everywhere. The minute it touches our boots the suction on the soles start to melt. Six of us have already fallen into the river of acid below. Our rays don't seem to affect it, and the mog gunner can't get into position for a clear shot. Whenever he gets close enough to fire, the cholent sprays out a steady stream of acid at him. We've lost the first and second gunner already. I'm still hoping we can keep the cholent busy so our last mog gunner will have a clear shot.

"There is one thing, though, Captain," Shimshon added, almost in a whisper. "Some of the beans on the cholent have turned a very dark, almost bluish color. They look like they're getting ready to burst."

"Get out of there, Nav Two. Get your men out!" screamed the captain. His screams froze everyone in the control center.

But for the men attacking the cholent, the warning came too late.

Those multis with the most noses were the first victims. The blue bubble-bursts sent out a new type of gas, a toxic gas, stronger even than shmertz. This was the gas that cholents used for emergency self defense. No known air filter could protect against this gas. Within moments, the multis closest to the cholent began screaming in agony as the gas penetrated their nostrils. The heavy high-grade filters were thrown off in a mad attempt by some multis to outrun the gases and acid. All for nothing.

The death cries of the multis lasted only minutes.

Captain Velgrayd had warned his men as soon as he realized the danger. This was the classic maneuver of the cholents on their home planet. The adult cholent would lure a beandragon by pretending to be sick. He would slowly burst only low sulphur bean gases. As the beandragon came closer, the cholent would release his most deadly blue bean gas, instantly choking the enemy to death.

At the Academy everyone learned about the *"blue bean bursts"* of the cholents. Everyone, that is, except Zuzstein. He had been busy getting married, thought the captain. Well, he should have waited.

"Victor," the captain commanded, sending his thoughts back to the computer, "was there enough time to analyze the gases or the acid?"

"Yes Captain," answered Victor. "The acid can be neutralized. The gases however, vary so greatly in density and weight that we will not be able to neutralize most of them within the time left us."

"Well at least we can stop the acid," Velgrayd announced to the men in the room. They did not look up, but continued, glumly, doing their work.

The captain abruptly stood up and walked over to his communications officer.

"Radio Command Central. Tell them our situation. Have them send a rescue ship from the nearest planet. Then open all frequencies and send an SOS. Make sure you mention the cholent. I don't want anyone else suffering our fate."

The ship suddenly lurched forward. The captain tried to grab onto something to steady himself. Unfortunately, there was nothing to grab except the

The death cries of the multis lasted only minutes.

communications officer. In what looked like a dance, the captain and his officer, holding onto each other, twirled around the control room as the ship tilted from side to side. Then, without warning, the spacecraft came to an abrupt halt.

Velgrayd and the communications officer, still locked together, tumbled onto the floor and rolled toward the center of the cabin where the captain's chair stopped them.

As the captain picked himself up, he saw dozens of hands covering dozens of mouths trying to hold back the sounds of laughter. So many hands could not cover so many mouths completely, and giggles, cackles, and laughter slowly filled the room.

At first, Velgrayd felt angry. Then he realized it was probably good that the men release some of their tension.

Then, listening for a moment, he suddenly felt fear. The noise of sirens and alarms that had filled the room until now was gone!

"Victor, what happened?" he bellowed. When he received no answer, he put on his privispeak, switched to the coded channel and thought, "What the Zombats happened, Victor?"

Silence answered his thoughts.

"Victor? What happened? Answer me," he mentally screamed. Rarely had the captain lost contact with the ship's computer.

Never during an emergency.

"So-r-ry Cap-tai-n," the computer finally responded. The captain felt like molasses was being spread within his brain.

"What's wrong Victor? You feel like you're in slow motion."

"Jus-ta min-u-te Cap-t-ain." Silence. "I had to rezap some of my lines," Victor said, now coming in loud and clear. "I have contained the acid flow, but it destroyed some of the Polton nodes that control a number of my motor functions. I am better now, Captain, except for some of my security warning systems."

"Forget about the security system," commanded the captain. "What happened to the ship? Why have we stopped?"

"That is the problem I am trying to work on now, Captain. Even as we talk I have located something in the engine room. There appear to be two intruders. They seem to have destroyed the plutonium rods. The engines are no longer operational."

Intruders! thought the captain. For the first time Velgrayd fully entertained the possibility that none of them would get out of this alive.

"Unfortunately," continued Victor, "the intruders have managed to eliminate most of my sensors in the engine room. Neither my ultra violet nor my gamma ray visuals are working now. I cannot see them."

"Who are these intruders?" the captain demanded to know.

"I have no record of a cholent being able to handle any machinery as complicated as our engines, Sir," Victor answered. "But I have no definite information that it can't. Therefore, it is my opinion that a second cholent and perhaps a humanoid have control of the engine room."

Captain Velgrayd gulped and then turned off the privispeak. Two cholents and an accomplice, he thought to himself.

We don't stand a chance.

Chapter 6
Acid And Antacid

The cholent had been in a gas frenzy, releasing large volumes of his deadliest gases in a magnificent display of purple and blue bean bubble-bursts. Blinded by the thick gases swirling around him, the Cholent could nevertheless sense the approach of the humanoids. His rage was so intense however, that he did not realize what he was doing to himself. The energy he was using to burst the giant blue beans was steadily draining his ability to burst his vital breathing beans. So, by the time the humanoids were dead, the exhausted cholent was almost dead as well.

For Shimshon, it was the cholent's near fatal mistake plus the fact that he had wisely stuffed his nose with oxytabs right before the attack, that saved his life. Unfortunately, even if the multis had thought to take oxytabs, there was little chance that all the tabs would work 100 per cent of the time in all their noses. And for them, even a small dose of blue bean gas meant instant death.

So, while the cholent lay shuddering, trying desperately to burst its beans in the proper breathing order, Shimshon approached it from the ceiling. By this time the antacid liquids being poured into the hold by the computer had begun doing their work. The cholent's acid was being neutralized and, soon, when the antacid reached the cholent itself, it too would be immobilized.

Watching the dying cholent, Zuzstein couldn't help feeling a sense of pity. He knew only too well what it meant to be an outcast. He could imagine what it meant to be the last of your kind. And he had learned about the cholents, not at the Academy, but in religious school.

The physical similarity of cholents to the traditional cholent Jews ate every Saturday for lunch, made the discovery of the planet Yapzug a topic of constant discussion to intergalactic Jewry. It also revived a tradition of cholent jokes that had been forgotten for centuries. But mostly Jews marvelled at the ability of God to take even man's jokes and turn them into something real.

When Yapzug was destroyed by the multis the Jews protested loudly, reminding the world, once again, what a holocaust could lead to. But by then the Holocaust was a history lesson, unreal to most people. So the Jewish protests fell on deaf ears, or ears which disliked Jews anyway.

It was the Jews who made sure the cholent was given a fair and open court trial. It was the Jews, more than any other group, who sensed the loneliness that filled the cholent. And it was the Jews who used their intergalactic connections to force the court to reach the verdict of exile rather than death. Even EFC, Exile From Civilization, seemed a ridiculous punishment for the simple sin of existing. But it was the best the Jews could do.

And now, here was the last cholent. Dying. In front of the Jew, Shimshon Zuzstein.

Shimshon knew his magneboots could keep him suspended from the roof of the room forever, but his oxygen was limited. His privispeak was not working and there were a number of acid holes already visible in his spacesuit. He would have to return to the captain and tell him what happened. Even now, the captain was probably sending another team to attack the cholent. Meanwhile, the antacid was hissing, creating little clouds of steam as it neutralized the streams of acid around the cholent.

The cholent jerked when the first drops of antacid burned its outer beans. It tried to move, but it was far slower than the acid. Without really thinking it out, Shimshon pressed the release on his magneboots, performed a routine floor flip, and landed, with a splash, right near the cholent.

Looking at the unpopped beans, filled with gases, his first thought was of the jelly beans he used to collect as a child. He would often scoop up fifty or so and make a pile on the kitchen table. Then he would begin cramming different colored beans together until he had packed them into a tight bean hill. He would glue these bean hills together. Hills of different heights were scattered all over his room.

Shimshon hesitated, then he touched the beans. Nothing happened. Slowly, he began pushing the cholent away from the antacid and toward the emergency exit that led into the engine room. He felt goose pimples running up and down his arms and on his back as he touched the leathery beans with his gloves.

He could never have shoved the cholent into the other room if not for the antacid. Each time a drop touched the cholent it slithered forward, dripping whatever acid it could to counter the effects of the antacid. This drip effect was becoming a serious danger for Shimshon. The cholent's acid, while not meant to attack him, was slowly dissolving additional parts of his outer clothing, and more importantly, his boots. If the acid touched any part of the inner lining of his clothes he would suffer major burns and possibly a very painful death.

Clouds of steam continued to fill the chamber. Shimshon kept pushing until the cholent was right next to the entrance. He hit the door open and the cholent slid into the engine room. He jumped in after the cholent and closed the door behind them.

Shimshon quickly removed his suit and outer helmet, and looked around. He was vaguely familiar with the workings of the engine room. Too late, he realized some acid from the cholent was burning the ship's main power supply. Before he could do anything, the ship began to rock violently back and forth.

The cholent, almost conscious now, felt the rocking, and imagined it to be an earthquake on Yapzug. He immediately scrunched up into a giant bean ball and began rolling. The engine room, while large, was filled with row after row of liquid titanium rods. The cholent crashed into dozens of these rods, bending and breaking them, and sending many of them flying into the air. Black and green liquid squirted out of the rods. After mowing down almost half of them, the cholent wedged himself under one of the control panels and stopped rolling.

Shimshon was not so lucky. Without his weight-suit and boots, he actually flew from one end of the room to the other. He used all his combat training to roll, flip, and land correctly. Fortunately, out of habit, he had kept on his inner helmet.

When enough liquid titanium leaked out of the rods, the ship came to an abrupt halt. The rods, like dozens of ninchucks, flew about the room banging and clanging on anything in their way. Shimshon felt like a karateki as he tried to block the flying rods.

One of the rods smashed the power base of the security field. Two others ripped apart the room's computer pods. Others bounced harmlessly off the cholent. By this time Shimshon had wisely sought cover behind a work-robot which now hung, broken and useless, from its iridium base.

A large rock crystal, used as solid fuel for the spaceship, was hit by a flying rod. It, in turn, flew high in the air above Shimshon. With a loud "thunk" it hit the wall behind him and landed on the back of his head. His inner helmet cracked, saving his life, but he was beginning to lose consciousness. Shimshon felt himself sucked into a black whirlpool that seemed to have no beginning and no end. Suddenly he was sure he heard the frightening sound of a blue cholent bean bursting.

But by then, of course, he didn't care.

Chapter 7
The Laz-cannon

The Starfarer lay crippled in space. The nearest planet was still over 5,000 light years away, and the nearest rescue vessel over 8 hours from contact.

Captain Velgrayd had been sure that if the ship could just maintain its speed, and control the damage done by the cholent, they would meet one of the rescue ships speeding toward them. Then it would be only a matter of transferring the crew to the other ship and happily watching as the rescue ship blasted the cholent to bite-size pieces.

But now, with their engines shut down, rescue was impossible.

"We have to fend for ourselves," the captain said, out loud.

"We seem to have stopped the cholent, but there

is an intruder in one of the engine rooms. He or it has done major damage. If we don't get a repair crew in there soon we'll have to wait days until rescue arrives. Obviously, we don't have enough antacid available to keep the cholent neutralized that long.

"We need two teams," Velgrayd announced. "Team A will attack the cholent. It should be able to get in close now that its acid is neutralized.

"Team B will attack the engine room. Whatever is in there must be destroyed, without doing additional damage to the engines."

The captain looked at his officers. He could see that each humanoid was considering the pros and cons of volunteering for either team. But Velgrayd was going to make their choice easier.

"Team A will be single-nosed volunteers only. Multis will make up Team B."

"But sir," Dwardher Kron, the stellar navigator, a human from Luna, began, "wouldn't it make more sense to split each group just in case there's another –"

"Quiet!" demanded the captain. He hadn't wanted the possibility of yet another cholent aboard brought out into the open. Now, thanks to Dwardher, he had to deal with it.

"Victor assures me there is no cholent in the engine room," the captain lied. "It may just be a robot gone haywire. Or sabotage. Or any one of a number of things. We won't know for sure until we break into the engine room. What I am sure about is that we have to eliminate whatever is controlling our engines. We also have to neutralize the cholent in the ship's main hold. We can't afford to lose more air. Victor, how much time do we have?"

"Approximately 4 point 3 hours sir," the computer answered, "if there is no further sabotage, and if the cholent does not release any additional large amounts of poisonous gases."

The captain turned to his stellar navigator. "Dwardher, since you seem to have a keen interest in the make-up of these groups, you can take Team A to destroy the cholent. I want you to take a laz-cannon, and our best laz-gunner with you."

Dwardher knew enough not to say anything more. The captain was not in an "any questions?" mood. But the navigator was scared beyond anything he had felt before. The cholent was one thing. The laz-cannon quite another.

A laz-cannon was used on a planet to clear obstacles – natural or man-made – that might hold up colonization or exploration. Its deadly energy destroyed soundlessly. It encircled any object in a sound warp. The sound disintegrated everything within it. The problem was that some of the sound beams rebounded back to the source of the power supply, the laz-cannon itself, destroying it and anyone around it. On large planets, laz-gunners were usually able to keep far enough from the object they were shooting at to ensure that the deadly beams would not be able to reach back at them. In a spaceship, however, when the laz-gunner fired he would in effect be signing a death warrant for himself — and those around him.

The two teams began their journey toward the belly of the spaceship. Information coming in from Victor seemed to indicate that as far as the main hold was concerned, the antacid had done its job.

"Perhaps," thought Dwardher, "the cholent is dead?"

"No!" came Victor's unasked-for reply.

Team B travelled vertically through the Starfarer to get to the engine room. This way they could check all lower levels just in case there were any more aliens aboard. But only drones whizzed by periodically, intent on some pre-programmed job.

When they arrived at the engine room's main door, Team B planted their first charges.

Dwardher and Team A entered the lower hold. He and his men found themselves sloshing through a small stream of what was now antacid. The laz-gunner left the group and moved ahead into the area where the cholent was supposed to be. In order to minimize possible rebound damage, the men were kept as far behind the laz-gunner as possible.

Everyone held their breath. But the silence was abruptly broken when the laz-gunner sputtered, "The cholent is gone!"

"Gone?!" Dwardher repeated, unable to believe he had heard correctly.

"Yes sir," the laz-gunner assured him. "But there are plenty of bodies here. It must have been a terrific fight. Only –"

"Yes?" prompted Dwardher.

"If they killed it, where is it?"

"Wait there," Dwardher commanded. He motioned the rest of the team to move forward.

"Tell me what you think happened as soon as you get to the scene," the captain told him after hearing his report. "It could not have escaped without us seeing it," he continued. "All our external sensors are working. They've been on since we first made contact with the cholent. Find out where it is. NOW!"

Dwardher rushed onward, pushing into the lead. As he entered the hold where the cholent was supposed to be he froze. A dozen bodies in inhuman positions, some showing severe acid burns, littered the small passageway. Multis who had ripped off their helmets and suits, insanely seeking clean air, had died almost before they had torn out their useless filters. Everywhere he looked there were multis. He understood now why the captain had chosen a human team to launch the second attack.

"Captain," Dwardher said, "we're showing some small amounts of gases but nothing serious or dangerous. If the cholent was here it has long since gone. There is a hole all along our outer hull. Perhaps it successfully evaded our sensors and escaped?"

"Impossible!" declared the captain. "Listen, either you are all drugged by those gases or it has managed to hide somewhere. Search out the entire hold. Check everywhere. Do it right away!"

"Yes sir," responded the navigator, relaying the message to his men. Before long they found the emergency door leading into the engine room. Dwardher was about to tell the captain what they had discovered when a giant explosion shook the spaceship and everyone screamed at once.

Team B was attacking.

Chapter 8
Traitor!

Shimshon woke up feeling queazy. He was sure he was experiencing the first effects of shmertz gas poisoning, or worse. He tried not to breathe in but after what seemed an eternity he took a deep breath and prepared to die.

Then, he felt a voice.

"Nosey!" the voice said, "Awaken!"

Absent-mindedly, and with his eyes still shut, Shimshon touched his nose.

"My nose is awake," he thought.

"What does that mean?" the voice asked. "I repeat. Nosey! Awake!"

Realizing he was still very much alive, Shimshon opened his eyes. There was very little light in the room. Most of the holobulbs had been smashed.

He stood up slowly and found the cholent still wedged in the corner.

A wave of nausea spread over him again.

"I feel it too," said the cholent. "Interspecie mind-link is most revolting. I hate to do it. But I have no choice."

"What is happening?" Shimshon said out loud. Then realizing the cholent could not hear him, he thought his question.

"We were under attack," responded the cholent within his mind. "You saved me. Although you had originally come to destroy me. So, we are even."

"I don't think I understand your logic," Shimshon thought.

-"It is logical," the cholent assured him. "Now we must continue to save me. In a short time I will have enough energy to leave or, if necessary, continue my attack. However, I shall try to further repay your service to me. As much as I am able, I will not direct my gases at you."

Shimshon did not feel at all relieved.

"Cholent," he thought, "if you release your gas anywhere in this room I will die."

"I understand," the cholent transmitted. Then it was silent for a moment. "I am sorry," it lamented. Then, without warning, the cholent sent images of its home planet, its capture, and its trial, through Shimshon's mind. The Nav Two couldn't help himself. He began to cry.

"I'm sorry for what happened to you," Shimshon sobbed. "My people have also suffered terrible carnage."

"Have other races attacked yours?" asked the cholent.

"No, our greatest threat has been from within; from us humans."

"That is hard to believe," the cholent said. "No species kills its own kind for long and survives."

"That's probably why the human race has begun to kill other species, like yourself," Shimshon answered.

As he was talking, Shimshon realized that he had to try and save the cholent. It gave him a good feeling, and yet a hopeless one as well.

"We must get you out of here and into deep space before another attack group arrives," he told the cholent. "When they see all the bodies outside they'll stop at nothing to destroy you. See if you can push your way out of those rods."

"It is no problem for me, I will just release some gas at my back end," the cholent explained.

"If you do that, I will die," Shimshon warned him.

The cholent sent a mental smile into the mind of Shimshon.

"This gas will not kill you, although it may be a bit unpleasant."

The cholent began bursting a few beans. The

smell of rotten eggs wafted throughout the cabin. Shimshon hated the smell but, sure enough, he saw it did him no real harm. Looking around he found his spacesuit. He reached into one of the pockets and found some air pellets. He stuck them up his nose and breathed fresh oxygen.

The cholent was across the room in no time and headed for the emergency door leading to the outside.

But an ear-splitting blast at the main door put an end to their plans for escape.

Team B came pouring through a hole that had once been the engine room door. At the same time, Team A, less dramatically, entered through the emergency door. Both teams faced each other, with the cholent and Shimshon between them.

Dwardher was the first to react.

"Don't fire. Anyone!" he yelled, just in time to stop the laz-gunner who seemed ready to open fire. One shot and they would all die.

"You," he pointed to Shimshon. "What are you doing here? How did you survive the cholent's attack? What's happening?"

Shimshon walked over to the cholent and rested both hands on him. The cholent shuddered for a moment, and then settled down.

"We can't kill him," Shimshon announced. "He's the survivor. The last of his kind. We can't kill him for defending himself."

"What are you talking about?" shouted Dwardher. "Did you see what he did to the multis out there?"

"Yes, I saw. I was there. But if you knew what our people have done to him, to his kind....Never mind! Look at this cholent. What do you see?"

No one seemed to understand him.

"Can't you see he's breathing. He's bursting beans. Watch," he smiled, bending over a bean as it burst. Instinctively, some multis turned their heads away. "I can stand next to him, inhale the gas and I'm still alive."

The multis of Team B began to mutter with all their mouths, creating an undercurrent of noise that Dwardher felt could be dangerous. They believed it was some sort of trick. They wanted to kill both the cholent and Shimshon. And they were ready to do so.

Dwardher knew he was way out of his league.

"Quiet!" he demanded. "The captain has been in touch with me. He's on his way. No one fires unless the cholent begins to burst his...shmertz beans."

"You still don't get it," Shimshon continued. "The cholent could kill me in a second if he wanted to. He could probably destroy most of us before we destroyed him. But that's just the point. He doesn't want to harm us. He just wants to leave."

"I can't allow that," Dwardher told Shimshon. "He has killed too many multis; too many of us.

We'll wait until the captain arrives and he'll decide what to do. Meanwhile, stay where you are," he warned Shimshon. "If you need a suit and helmet we will provide one."

Shimshon didn't answer. They all waited in silence. Occasionally, a bean would burst, someone would raise their laser, and, after seeing Shimshon safe and unaffected, would try to relax.

The captain entered the room and took charge at once.

"Arrest that man," he ordered the officers behind him, pointing at Shimshon.

The officers made a move toward Shimshon, but when they saw he was touching the cholent they stopped in their tracks. They were afraid. More than afraid – they were terrified!

The captain felt he had no choice. He would handle the mutiny later. Right now he needed to handle this Jew. It was just as he had expected. A traitor. The old song was right. One less Jew would make everyone happier.

He rushed over to Shimshon, grabbed his cloak and ripped him away from the cholent. Shimshon, his hands clenched, fought for control.

"You!" the captain yelled. "Now you're helping cholents to destroy humans! Were you a spy for this monstrosity right from the beginning? Did you lead those multis into a death trap? Did you, Jew?" the captain spat. He threw Shimshon in the waiting arms of the officers who were still a safe distance from the cholent. They marched him immediately to the brig, happy to be out of the room.

The moment Shimshon left the room, the cholent, the last of his kind, shot a stream of acid directly at the captain. The force of the acid wave toppled the captain, but he was dead almost before he touched the ground. The deadly acid seared through the captain's spacesuit and burned him beyond recognition.

Dwardher couldn't take any more.

"Fire!" he shouted.

Then he realized, too late, that the laz-gunner would automatically obey. The silence of the laz-cannon was overpowering. The cholent was baked, then fried, then turned into bean ash. Dwardher and his men had just enough time to enjoy their victory before the energy wave bounced off the surrounding walls and disintegrated them. In seconds, only a thin film of ash was left on the floor of the engine room.

When the rescue craft, Bismol II, finally arrived to save the men of the Starfarer, everyone was already dead. Their oxygen had long since run out.

Victor had recorded the last minutes of everyone, including the Jew, Shimshon Zuzstein.

The computer had noted that a shuttlecraft had

He rushed over to Shimshon, grabbed his cloak and
ripped him away from the cholent.

taken off, illegally, from the Starfarer almost immediately after the captain and the attack teams had been destroyed. It was headed for a dead planet; a planet where no humanoid could survive.

Bismol II left the Starfarer and headed for its next rendezvous in the Ganymede quadrant. It was no use chasing a suicide into space. Let him die his way, the captain of the rescue craft thought.

Chapter 9
Ancient Jewish Tradition

When Shimshon landed on Yapzug the shuttle-craft was almost out of fuel. The planet itself was burned and lifeless. It was not the kind of place he would have chosen to die in, but it would have to do.

He took some beans out of his spacesuit. These were beans the cholent had pushed into his hands when Shimshon had touched him. Their mind-link had been unbroken up until the moment the cholent had died. He knew what he had to do.

Ancient Jewish tradition required he carry out the last will of a dying being.

From another pocket Shimshon removed some ptators. He had taken them from the Starfarer's well-stocked kitchen. Shimshon covered the beans with the ptators. In time, as they fed off the ptators, they would grow and leave the planet. It would be dangerous for them, but it was at least a chance for survival.

Anyway, Shimshon the Jew had kept his promise to the cholent. Now he laid down and waited for his oxygen to give out.

Before long he grabbed his stomach, almost doubling over. He looked at his oxygen gauge. Strange, he thought, I still have two hours of oxygen left.

Then, still clutching his stomach, he laughed out loud. He realized what was bothering him. It was another ancient Jewish tradition.

Gas.